MASTER BY CHOICE

A PUPPY PLAY ROMANCE

M.A. INNES

1

COOPER

"If you don't stop bouncing around, I'm going to tell Master you've been good today!" Sawyer's words burst out once he seemed to reach the end of his rope.

I was excited, but nowhere near hyper enough to be sending his stress levels that high. I'd have been worried, but I knew exactly what was on his mind. Giving him a big smile that made him groan in frustration, I answered him sweetly. "If you do, I'll tell him you were jerking off in the shower this morning."

His eyes went wide, but I could see the desire flaring in his eyes. "That's lying! I did not!"

"It doesn't matter. It will still get you the punishment you want." I had to laugh as Sawyer sputtered and sent me dirty looks. "I think he'll believe me enough that you could find yourself bent over his lap later."

And even though I'd be lying, Sawyer wouldn't be able to deny it convincingly enough, because he wanted the spanking.

Desperately.

"That's just..." Sawyer couldn't seem to find the word and drive at the same time.

"Perfect? Devious? Sexy as hell? I know." Beaming, I did a little happy dance in my seat. "If we weren't heading for such a perfect date, I'd say I couldn't wait to get home to Jackson's."

Sawyer still hadn't found his brain, so I went back to my original topic. "The amusement park, Sawyer! I haven't been in years. Do you think they still have the roller coaster that goes upside down?"

He just stared out the windshield, so I kept babbling. It wasn't hard. I was so excited they were going to have to peel me off the roof of the car. "It seemed scary last time I went, but I was young. So it probably—"

"You get sick riding in the back seat of the car. I'm not going to put you on a roller coaster!" Sawyer tried to calm down, but it wasn't working. He needed a spanking and wasn't admitting to Master just how much he wanted it. He sighed and tried to relax. "I'm sorry."

Reaching over, I let my hand rest on his leg. "Deep breath. We're just going to have fun and then go back and have hot sex. It's a stress-free day."

Sawyer finally laughed. "You're right. It's not the rides I'm worried about."

Duh.

I nodded, giving him an understanding look that was totally hammed up. "It's the hot sex later, isn't it?"

Shaking his head, Sawyer played the game with me. "Nope."

"The amount of sugar I'm going to consume?" That was definitely a good one.

"No." Then he started to laugh. "I can't believe he promised you all that shit."

"Master loves me. Of course he'd get me treats." *Oops.*

"Cooper—"

Not wanting the "We don't want to go too fast" lecture, I jumped in. "Watching me play as a pup? He promised me a surprise soon."

"No, but that should probably worry me." Then he sighed, and I knew I hadn't distracted him well enough. "I know how you feel, but we've only been on a couple of dates with him."

"Dates, shmates." I shrugged. "He likes my pup, and he's Master, and he buys me pancakes for dinner. Oh, and don't forget the hot sex." Couldn't leave that off the list. He was perfect, and I wasn't going to look for every reason it might not work.

"But—"

"Nope, no buts." We were not going down that road again. My worrywart. "He liked cuddling you while I played, and the sex was fabulous—did I forget to mention that part? And he liked going out with you for dinner. He doesn't mind that we do things at our own pace. Jackson's not trying to rush us."

Jackson was the perfect master, even if everything was new to him. He asked good questions and researched different things about BDSM and puppy play. It was clear he was taking our needs seriously and doing his best to be a good master and boyfriend. He was so earnest it was cute sometimes.

Sawyer nodded, not able to argue with any of my perfectly reasonable points. Until he started worrying about me being right. "But what if he doesn't rush us, and I go too slow?"

Lord, his mind must be an exhausting place to live.

"Does it seem like he's trying to take things so slow they don't go anywhere?" I thought it was a little silly, but I was going to let him figure it out.

"No, not exactly."

"We've had fabulous sex and have been on dates and he's seen my pup…" *What else…what else…?* "We all talk on the phone a lot, and he gives the best phone sex. Even when he says you can't touch yourself while he's talking."

He was perfect when it came to torturing me with pleasure.

Sawyer's head whipped around to look at me before he remembered he was driving. "He what?"

"You guys don't do that?" I shrugged. Evidently not, judging by the look on his face. "He does it when I'm home in the morning after you've gone to work. The first time, he said I was being naughty trying to distract him with dirty texts—and he was right—but that's not the point. Wait, what was the question?"

I tried to retrace my mental steps, but it was difficult because I was so excited. Jackson was right…naughty things… "Oh, dirty talk. Yes, well, he made me lie down on the bed, naked, and I wasn't allowed to touch myself while he jerked off and said all kinds of fabulous things. Best denial ever."

Sawyer was listening intently, so I dropped my voice and tried to make it sound sexy. "You know…if you hint to him that you'd like it, I know he'd do it with you too. He didn't just talk about the things he was going to do to me. Master had me listen while he described everything he was going to do to you too."

Best morning ever—even if I hadn't gotten to come.

"He would…I mean, he did?" Sawyer's mind seemed so distracted; I was starting to think I should have driven. But since we were almost there, it didn't matter anymore.

"Oh, yes. Master doesn't want to push you, but he loves telling me how sexy you are and how incredible we are together. Master's going to want to watch us do more things. I think it's hot. And don't even bother trying to deny it. I remember every naughty fantasy you've shared too."

Sawyer blushed. "I wasn't going to say anything like that."

Oh yes, he was. "You're worrying too much. He's doing his best to get to know us and to show us he's not just in it as a fling."

Sawyer's nod was slow, but he didn't try to deny that either. As we exited off the interstate and turned toward the park, he seemed to relax more. Finally, he started to speak on his own without me having to prod him. "Jackson said he wanted to go out later this week when you had to work late. He said something about going to get sushi or maybe trying that new steak place."

"Eww, the steak place, please. Do not come home smelling like fish and expect sex. Raw fish is gross." A shudder went through me at the thought. It was expensive enough that Sawyer didn't want it that often, but the one time he'd made me eat it, all I could remember was the way the green wrap thing stuck in my teeth and the feel of the fish. "Yuck."

He was nearly doubled over laughing as we pulled into the parking lot and started driving around in circles looking for a space. "I don't know why you hate it so much. It's good."

"The taste…the look…the texture…it's raw, dead stuff. Please, I could keep going." He was ruining my good mood. "No more talk of terrible things. Just sexy talk and fun talk today. That's the rule."

"Your rule, huh?" Sawyer's smile turned a little predatory as he finally found parking. I didn't care where we ended up, but he was one of those people who took glee in getting the best spot. He was insane, but I loved him anyway.

"Yes. I have the best rules." Smirking as he turned off the car, I looked around to see where we were and started texting Jackson as fast as my fingers would go. Speech-to-text wouldn't work for this one.

When the reply came back in seconds, I knew he was as excited as we were. "He's like three rows that way. As long as this alphabet system they've got going is really in ABC order."

"Why wouldn't it be in order?"

"Because people are insane and overorganize things. Don't you remember that fancy grocery store? Beans in like five different places." I shook my head. "And who separates condiments by what kind of meal they go with?"

As we got out of the car, I looked around and saw Jackson heading our way with a big smile on his face. "We're over here!"

Apparently, I was too loud or too excited or too *something* for Sawyer. He groaned, and I knew he was rolling his eyes. "Coop…"

"Yes, you are here. And judging by the look on Sawyer's face, you've been driving him crazy." Jackson grinned as he pulled me into his arms and gave me a deep kiss.

When he finally pulled back and I could catch my breath, I nodded. "He needed it."

His eyes were laughing, but I got a pointed stare. "So I have one pup who's driving the other nuts deliberately." Then he looked over at Sawyer. "And I have another who's worrying about something but doesn't want to talk about it?"

I nodded, and Sawyer blushed but didn't deny it. Jackson shook his head, like we were two very naughty pups, and my dick started to perk up and take notice. I liked that look. Jackson glanced back and forth between us. "I think I have two boys who need to be punished later."

"Oh, yes…" That sounded a little too eager, so I tried again. "I mean, I'm sorry we were bad, Master. I understand if we need to be punished."

Sawyer groaned, and his head fell back like he was praying for patience. "I'm going to take that damned phone away from you."

Grinning, I gave Jackson a smacky kiss, pressing myself even tighter against him since there weren't many people around. "I can't wait to go in."

He laughed, and his hips rocked forward to push his cock against mine. "You clearly can't wait for a lot of things."

"You're right." I wasn't going to hide how much I wanted him. "But I'll be good in the park. Promise."

Jackson shook his head and reached up to cup my face. "I don't believe that for a second. Just don't do anything to get us kicked out."

I gave him a pout I knew was cute. "Well, that limits all my fun. But I still get my treats, don't I?"

Sawyer was laughing and finally came around the back of the car to stand by Jackson. "How much sugar did you promise him?"

Jackson shrugged but gave Sawyer a wicked grin. "Just enough to make sure I'd get to punish him tonight."

I *knew* he was perfect.

I stretched up and gave him another quick kiss. "You're the best master ever."

His hand slid up to ruffle my hair, and his expression changed to something sweeter. "Thank you, Cooper."

Finally deciding that Sawyer was still entirely too nervous, I stepped back and reached out to grab his hand. "Hurry up and say hello to Master, so I can go on the rides."

Sawyer couldn't seem to decide if he was still nervous

over how serious I was getting, worried that he'd disappoint Jackson, turned-on over the thought of a spanking, or overwhelmed by the idea of having to wait all day, because he gave Jackson a bashful look and a thousand expressions flashed across his face. Deciding to help, I kept talking. "He's very excited."

Jackson wrapped one hand around Sawyer's waist and pulled him close, so they were pressed together just as tightly as we'd been. Some masters would have probably argued with instructions, but I loved the way Jackson just took my helpful little hints in stride.

"I'm very excited too. Aren't you?" Listening to Jackson's sexy voice, I had a feeling neither of them was talking about the amusement park as Sawyer nodded.

It was about time.

Jackson slowly leaned down and brushed his lips against Sawyer's, gently, like they were in a romance novel or something. Then he pulled back and even though I was at the wrong angle to get the full view, I could see his hand slide down to cup Sawyer's ass.

It was lucky we were hidden between the cars, or I wouldn't have been the one to get us all in trouble.

Jackson leaned down and whispered something to Sawyer. I only caught a part of it, a teasing remark about how sexy he was going to look before Jackson's voice went low again. It was probably reassurances that they wouldn't go too fast or a reminder that he had a safeword to stop or slow down if they needed to, because Sawyer nodded and smiled, looking a lot less nervous than when we'd gotten out of the car.

One last kiss, that time on the cheek, and Jackson pulled away. "Are we ready?"

I was more than ready…for everything. Spankings, cotton candy, roller coasters…well, maybe not the roller coaster. Sawyer might be right about that part. Grinning madly, I bounced up and down. "Yes!"

"He's definitely going to need to be spanked first." Sawyer probably meant because of how naughty I was going to be, but I thought it was a great idea.

"Me first!"

Jackson just laughed. "You, my sweet pup, are going to be a handful."

I batted my eyes at him. "But this handful still gets cotton candy, right?"

Sawyer knocked his shoulder into mine. "Come on, no more flirting."

"I did not promise that at all." I'd promised not to get us kicked out of the park.

There was a big difference.

2

SAWYER

"Do you really think that's a good idea?" Watching Cooper eat was giving me a stomachache, but when he started eyeing another cotton candy, it was time to draw the line.

"But…" He gave Jackson a pouting took.

Jackson shook his head like we were both silly and leaned close to whisper in Cooper's ear. Whatever he said was probably dirty, but it kept Cooper from begging for more sugar, so I was grateful. Cooper just grinned and gave me a wicked look before nodding. "Yes, Master."

Yup, dirty.

Jackson didn't seem to mind. He smiled at Cooper and reached out to cup his cheek. "Don't drive Sawyer nuts."

Cooper didn't even bother to hide what he was doing. "But it's sooo much fun."

Laughing, Jackson gave him a look like Cooper was the funniest thing he'd ever seen. "But you're already getting a spanking tonight. If you push Sawyer too far, he might not want to play with us later."

Play?

Like puppy or spanking?

Cooper sighed. "I didn't promise to be good. Besides, Sawyer loves me." Cooper leaned into Jackson's touch but peeked over at me and blew me a kiss. It wasn't terrible as far as PDAs went, but the lady standing beside us waiting for her chance to order blinked wide, and her mouth fell open.

She'd either been eavesdropping or had a dirty mind, because we hadn't been that bad.

"Come on." I tilted my head, trying to point out the nosy woman. "Let's drag him away before he makes himself sick."

"No fun." Cooper straightened but started cleaning up his mess from the cotton candy. I thought he was going to behave, but as he stood up, he leaned close to Jackson and kissed his cheek. "I'll be a good boy." Then the minx leaned over and kissed mine.

Shocked didn't even begin to describe her face.

But any guilt I felt fell away when instead of spewing religious shit at us, she just brought out her cell phone and took our picture. Some people had no boundaries.

Cooper loved it. He beamed and giggled as we all stood up and started walking away. I thought we were in the clear, but then he looked back over his shoulder, whispering loudly. "It's even better than you're imagining."

Lord.

I was going to kill him.

Jackson wasn't helping the situation either. He laughed and brought his hand up to ruffle Cooper's hair like he was a cheeky little sub, not a naughty slut who needed a spanking.

Wait.

Damn it. Either way, the shit got what he wanted.

Shaking my head, I herded them away before we ended

up YouTube sensations or worse, a Facebook meme. "You make me crazy."

Jackson reached out and cupped my face, seemingly unconcerned about the show of affection. "He keeps us on our toes."

I hadn't been sure how everything would work on our date. It wasn't so much worrying about how we would get along or if he had the patience for an excited Cooper, but it was the little things that made me nervous: affection in public...how to hide that we weren't just three friends hanging out...how to open up and ask for what I wanted.

Little things.

Tiny.

But so fucking big.

Cooper must have sensed my worries. He reached out and grabbed my hand, smiling sweetly. "Let's go do one more roller coaster."

"With your full stomach? Hell no. Let's go do the bumper cars again." He might not barf on those.

Jackson was laughing again. "I'm going to have to agree with Sawyer, pup. I'm not taking you on another roller coaster with all that sugar in your stomach."

Cooper started to pout, but a yawn ruined the effect. I wasn't surprised he was tired. He'd been up since first thing and had bounced all the way to the park. Spending hours wandering around and running from one ride to the next would have exhausted anyone.

"Okay, bumper cars. But we can come back another time and do more roller coasters?"

"Of course. We can even get season passes if we want to." Jackson said it like it was nothing big, but to me, the words were significant.

"Yes!" Cooper's eyes lit up, and he grinned. He could

see the long-term meaning in the words, and the minx wanted another excuse to act like a nut and get more sugar.

"All right, then. We'll talk about it with the park people on the way out. Most of the time, you get a discount at these kinds of places when you upgrade at the park." Steering us toward our new destination, he laughed as Cooper bounced forward to look at a stand selling stuffed animals.

Jackson took my hand and gave it a squeeze as he watched Cooper. "He's exhausted."

"He was up at the crack of dawn."

"I knew I should have had you guys stay over." He let his shoulder bump into mine.

"Between his job and your family, it would have been hard to make it all work. He's just going to sleep all the way home, anyway."

Jackson gave me a grin, and I rewound what I'd said.

Oh.

We were going back to Jackson's immediately after the park. Blushing, I glanced away to see Cooper pulling out his wallet to try to win a stuffed puppy by throwing rings at a moving belt of glass bottles.

Jackson chuckled. "He knows those are rigged, right?"

"Yes, but he's going to spend five bucks attempting to anyway." He had to. Cooper had this innate belief that all he had to do was keep trying, and it would work out. It'd kept us going through long nights, but sometimes it was overwhelming.

"It's what makes Cooper unique." Then Jackson leaned close and pressed a kiss to my head. "But we're not trying to keep up with him or compete in any way. We all do things at our own pace. Right?"

Cooper had tattled.

"Yes." But I didn't like my own worries holding me back. "But—"

When I couldn't finish the sentence, Jackson took over. "But sometimes we need help to give us a push?"

The answer came out quietly, but I was proud that I didn't hesitate. "Yes."

"That's all I had to hear." Jackson spoke confidently, like he knew exactly what needed to happen, and his calm demeanor soothed the jumble of emotions inside of me. "Now, come on. Let's figure out how to win him a puppy before he spends a fortune on that thing."

"I'd wish you luck, but I'm not sure that would help." I shook my head as Cooper refused to give up.

"I don't need any more luck. I've got plenty."

He must have seen my confusion, because he gave me a tender smile. "I found you two, didn't I?"

I'D BEEN RIGHT; FIVE MINUTES INTO THE DRIVE AND HE'D been out. With the stupid stuffed dog as his pillow. I really didn't need any more alone time with my thoughts, but the ride to Jackson's gave me plenty.

Grumbling low, while Cooper shifted and made quiet little noises, I tried to get comfortable. "I don't care how crazy the schedules are to match up. The next time we go anywhere together, we're taking one car."

By the time I pulled into Jackson's driveway, I was tired, hungry, and curious about the rest of our night. Food that didn't list sugar as the first ingredient was my main priority, but I had a feeling sex was going to be Cooper's.

I just wasn't sure about Jackson.

The look he'd given Cooper as he'd said good-bye to him had been heated and wicked. When he'd turned that heat toward me, it hadn't faded, but it had turned sweeter, and I could see a confidence in his eyes that wasn't always there.

Whatever Cooper had texted him, I was glad it made Jackson feel better. I hated that I was the reason he worried about what was happening between us. In a warped way, though, it made me feel better. Just knowing he was thinking about us, and about the future, made it easier for me to admit how attached I was growing to him.

Cooper was beyond attached. He was head over heels in love with Master, and the only thing that held him back from jumping around telling Jackson at the top of his lungs was me. I couldn't decide if he was rushing or if it was just the way he was. Cooper went into everything full speed ahead, and love seemed to be the same way for him.

Had it been the same way for us?

Once I'd gone from being his friend to being his family, had it been the same way? I never questioned how he felt about me. He'd said the words, and I could see them in his eyes. Looking back, I couldn't really say how long it had taken before he told me he loved me.

I remembered wrapping myself around him in that dingy little motel room and holding on to him for dear life. I remembered knowing we would be together forever and telling him how much I loved him, but I couldn't say if it had been days or weeks after we'd moved in together.

Did it matter?

As I glanced over at Cooper, curled up against the car door, relaxed and beautiful, I wasn't sure it did. I knew he loved me, and I knew we were tied together forever. But I also knew that there was room in our lives for someone else, someone like Jackson.

We didn't need a Dom to keep us on track, and we didn't need someone to make decisions for us. We were pretty damned functional and had accomplished a lot since we'd first left home. But having him there was relaxing and soothing in a way that nothing else was.

There was nothing to worry about, and nothing that was up to me. Cooper's pleasure…my pleasure…Cooper playing as a pup…punishments…none of it was my responsibility any longer. Every time I thought about completely submitting to Jackson, it sent a wave of need and nerves through me.

I'd dated and fucked enough guys in high school to know I was submissive. I knew the types of things I wanted to explore, and Cooper had opened my eyes to even more, but there was a difference between a bit of rough sex that made someone curious and true submission.

What I wanted with Jackson was so much more than just bottoming while he slapped my ass a couple of times. But it was that desire for more that made me wary. Cooper had spanked me before, and he caressed me while I was a pup, and he was an aggressive top when he needed to be, but that wasn't the same.

Or maybe it was, and I was just a worrywart—as Cooper liked to tease.

If I ended up with Wart as my pup name, I was going to kill him.

Finally turning off the car, I reached over and rubbed Cooper's leg. "Coop, we're back at Jackson's now."

He shifted and scrunched his face up. "We're home?"

Basically, yes.

"No, we're at Jackson's, remember? We were going to stay here tonight." We'd all agreed that after the long day at the park and then dinner and hanging out, we probably wouldn't have the energy to go back to our place.

Well, that had been the excuse we'd used to justify sleeping over with Jackson—not that Cooper had needed one. He loved staying at Jackson's, and he didn't bother to play hard to get…and I had to admit, I didn't either. Even though we'd only known him a short while, relaxing at his house, even if we didn't do anything sexual, felt natural.

However, Cooper made sure that something sexual always happened. Not that we'd had that many dates yet in the two weeks since that first meeting—but Cooper was doing his best to get me more comfortable. I couldn't decide if I appreciated his version of "helping" or not.

Jackson finally gave up waiting for us to get out of the car, and he walked over toward my side and opened the door. Bending over, he looked in. "Is he still sleeping?"

I nodded while Cooper shook his head, eyes still closed, and grumbled. "No. I'm here."

Jackson grinned and leaned close. In a bad stage whisper, he spoke again. "Does he know that here and awake are not the same thing?"

I shrugged, playing along. "That's a very good question. I'm not sure. You might have to do some investigation to see if he's really awake or just talking in his sleep."

Trying to hold back his laughter, Jackson leaned over me and reached through the car. Letting his fingers trail over Cooper's groin, Jackson did his best to sound serious. "I think he's dead. His cock isn't hard."

"Yup. He's always hard. If he's soft, he must have kicked the bucket. It's very sad." I gave Jackson a quick kiss. "Does that mean I get to eat his portion of dessert?"

At that, Cooper decided playing possum might not be the best idea any longer. "Dessert?"

Jackson and I laughed as Cooper looked up at the house. "What did you get?"

"Nothing." Jackson gave Cooper's cock one last teasing caress and then moved back to stand up. "You've had enough junk today."

Cooper pouted. "But, Master, I was so good."

Shaking his head, Jackson ignored the sexy expression. "Dinner and then we'll relax. Sawyer, I grabbed that action movie you were talking about, so we can see if it's any good if you want to."

Pleased that he'd remembered, I unbuckled and started climbing out of the car. Giving Jackson another peck, I smiled. "Thank you. I can't wait to see it. Lots of mixed reviews but as long as they didn't show all the good parts in the trailers, it should be great."

Once Cooper decided that being awake was a better option, he didn't waste any time jumping out of the car. "What's for dinner?"

I might not be as bouncy as Cooper, but I was just as curious. Jackson had said he was going to teach us to cook new things, but there hadn't been enough time yet. "I think we were promised something delicious."

Cooper managed to get his excitement under enough control to grab the bag out of the trunk, but then he came dancing around the side and threw himself at Jackson. "I'm starving."

Jackson wrapped his arms around Cooper, grinning. "How can you be hungry? You ate about every hour today."

Cooper beamed at him. "I'm just special that way." Then giving Jackson a passionate kiss, he pulled back, breathless. "All this fabulous excitement takes lots of energy."

"Fabulous excitement, huh?"

"Yes, and I'm going to need lots of energy for later." Cooper wiggled his eyebrows up and down, lecherously.

"I'm not sure you need lots of energy for watching a movie. I think that's quiet and relaxing." Jackson tried to keep a straight face while he said it, but the laughter in his eyes ruined it.

Cooper wasn't going to let him even tease about something that horrible. "Oh, no. I was promised a spanking if I was good. I was perfect today, and that means spankings and incredible sex."

I snorted. "You almost gave that one couple a heart attack when you grabbed Jackson's ass."

Cooper stuck out his tongue at me. "They shouldn't have been gossiping."

Jackson choked back a laugh. "And what about the lady in line?"

Shrugging, Cooper blinked up innocently. "I don't remember any lady."

"You have a very selective memory, my boy. Come on, let's go inside. Dinner's almost ready." Jackson gave Cooper a pat on the ass, urging him into the house, before reaching out to take my hand. "You were very good today, but I don't think I remember what you wanted for a treat."

Because I wasn't a nut who needed to be bribed to function or a flirt who liked pushing the limit.

"Um, a treat?" So maybe that wasn't the best answer.

Jackson's smile turned tender. "How about I give you what I think you want?" His free hand came up to cup my cheek. "Something you need but haven't talked about yet."

Stupid tattletale.

"Um…"

Cooper thought it was so perfect he was nearly wagging his nonexistent tail as he waited on the porch. "Yes, Master! That would be a great idea! Sawyer was very good too today. He didn't even get frustrated with me at all."

Because Jackson had been there to keep the little minx in line. It was easier to relax when it wasn't my responsibility. It was really too bad I couldn't think of a good reason for Jackson to go grocery shopping with us too. It would probably save us a ton on impulse purchases.

And I was trying to find any excuse in the world not to think about what might happen later.

"Thank you, Master." It wasn't quite admitting what I wanted out loud, but I wasn't going to lie to him or myself. Taking a deep breath, I stepped closer and curled into him.

Closing my eyes for just a moment, I pushed the nerves away. I wanted this. I wanted Jackson. I wanted to see where everything would go. I wanted to hear the words come from him one day. I wanted to see his face light up when Cooper said the words to him.

I wanted so much it was frightening.

3

JACKSON

My sweet boy.
    And my crazy boy.

Cooper seemed to be content bouncing around the porch, so I didn't feel guilty about focusing on Sawyer. I resisted the urge to ask something stupid…especially when I knew the answers.

Yes, he was okay.

No, he didn't want me to back off.

Yes, he really wanted to be spanked and to submit.

No, he wasn't going to ask for it.

Yes, he knew his safewords.

No, he wasn't going to kill Cooper for tattling on him.

That last one might have been a stretch. "Let's go inside and get you some food, then we'll cuddle up with the movie."

For a while.

Leaving that part unspoken didn't seem to help Sawyer's nerves, but his head went up and down against my chest as he nodded. Holding him until he was ready to move, I kept talking. "I put stew in the Crock-Pot earlier.

Do you think he has the patience for me to make biscuits to go with it?"

Sawyer laughed, low and sweet. "Probably not, but I want them, so he's going to have to wait."

"Oh, have I found something that you like?" I learned more about them every time we talked or did something together, but it still gave me a zing of pleasure when I found something new.

His head nodded again. "We've only made the ones in the can work...and that's not really the same."

I pretended to stagger and groaned. "Don't say things like that to the old man—you'll give me a heart attack... canned biscuits. That's just...I don't even have the words for how horrifying that is."

Laughing, Sawyer pulled away enough to look up at me. "So...I shouldn't tell you that we managed to burn the outside but somehow leave the inside almost raw with those peel-apart ones?"

I gave Sawyer a dramatic shudder and looked over at Cooper who was shaking his head like we were insane. "Cooper, you have to save me. He's trying to kill me."

Cooper sighed. "You can't kill him. I haven't gotten sex in days...or a spanking. I need him first."

Giving Sawyer a wink, I took a step back. "I think Cooper needs attention."

Cooper's eyes widened in excitement, but Sawyer gave me a knowing look. He was clearly much more suspicious than Cooper. Turning quickly, I made it up the stairs of the porch before Cooper could decide what to do.

Sawyer was laughing as I wrapped my arms around Cooper, and he squeaked out in surprise. "Someone is being very naughty. Keep me alive until you get sex, huh?"

"That's what Sawyer said, not me." Cooper was

laughing breathlessly, trying to get out of the hole he'd dug for himself.

"Trying to throw Sawyer under the bus?" Before he could answer, I dug my fingers into his sides and started tickling him while he howled with laughter. "To save yourself or to get a spanking?"

There was no way Cooper could actually form a sentence, but I kept up the pretense of needing an answer simply to justify "punishing" him. "Refusing to answer me, huh? Throwing Sawyer under the bus, all that sugar today, only needing me around for sex? Yes, I think I have a boy in desperate need of a punishment."

Cooper was still laughing too hard to respond with more than just single words, but he nodded enthusiastically as I tickled him. "Please…yes…yes…"

Pinning him tightly against me, I stopped my fingers long enough for him to catch his breath. "That doesn't mean I'm going to spank you, though. You'd like that too much, my naughty pup."

"Oh, but Master…" Cooper pouted but ruined his pathetic look by rubbing his cock against my thigh. "I need —"

"Sex and a spanking…I heard."

Cooper looked up at me, so innocent and sweet, shaking his head. "Oh, no Master…I just need you."

He was so cute it was almost perfect.

But I knew better than to believe him — at least about most of it. The emotion was genuine. I could see in his eyes how much I was starting to mean to him, but there was also that layer of fake innocence that was all naughty Cooper.

Sawyer evidently wanted to make sure I didn't fall for it, because he snorted. "Master's too smart to fall for that act. Try again."

Cooper turned his head and stuck his tongue out at

Sawyer, then turned back to focus those wide, innocent eyes on me. He was damned good at that "I'm so sweet" routine. It made all the things I wanted to do to him even more wicked.

Leaning down, I licked around his ear while I whispered. "Are you going to look that sweet and innocent while I'm fucking you and spanking that sexy ass of yours? Do you want to play the virgin that gets thoroughly debauched by the big, rough villain?"

I thought the idea was hot, and Cooper just melted into my arms, knees going rubbery while he moaned. "Ohh, Master."

Giving him a devilish grin as I pulled away, I kissed him tenderly. "Then I think you're going to have to keep me around for longer than just a spanking and sex."

Cooper gave me a slightly drunken nod. "Yes…oh, yes…"

Laughing at us both, Sawyer finally came up onto the porch, shaking his head. "I think you broke him."

Wiggling my eyebrows up and down, I leered at Sawyer. "I did."

"I'm not even going to ask what you said to him." Shaking his head, Sawyer poked us both in the sides. "Feed me. I was promised dinner."

Reaching out, I pulled Sawyer close, trapping him there with my arm. "I think I promised you all kinds of things tonight."

As he blushed but didn't deny it, I leaned down and kissed him gently. Pulling back, I whispered low. "And the first thing I promised you…" Sawyer's expression was heated but nervous as I paused, dragging out the silence. "…was biscuits."

"You're terrible." He laughed, probably relieved that I wasn't going to talk about his spanking at the moment.

Cooper, on the other hand, grinned. "Biscuits? You're really going to make them? Like from scratch?"

Cooper's excitement was contagious, and smiling at him, I nodded. "Yes. Do you want to learn how to do it?"

"Yes!" Cooper was nearly bouncing in my arms, so I gave his ass a pat and let him go.

"All right, then. We need to get started, so we can feed Sawyer. I can't have my boys starving to death before we get to the fun part of the evening."

Sawyer's blush deepened, but Cooper started dancing around and chanting. "I'm getting a spanking...I'm getting a spanking..."

Rolling his eyes, Sawyer gave Cooper a frustrated look as I started to open the door. Cooper didn't seem to mind a bit; he just grinned even wider. "Come on, you know you're just as excited."

"Come on, you two. Dinner." Not wanting Sawyer to get any more upset, I looked at Cooper. "Behave."

Neither confirming nor denying the sexy accusation, Sawyer headed into the house. Herding everyone into the kitchen, I had Sawyer dishing out the stew, so it could cool as Cooper and I made the biscuits. Cooper was just as excitable making the biscuits as he was doing everything else, and I was starting to get an idea of how they'd killed the other ones.

But before long, the meal was ready, and we were relaxing around the table. A cloud of flour and some sticky countertops in his wake, Cooper thoroughly pleased with his creations, even if they were slightly misshapen.

"This one looks like a dick...a tiny, slightly lumpy one." What made Cooper's words even funnier was how serious his expression became—right before popping the whole thing into his mouth.

Frowning at him, I shook my head. "You're going to choke."

Sawyer's response came out dry and perfectly timed. "Not on a dick that small."

Cooper thought it was so funny, he started to laugh. Unfortunately, it was midswallow, so he started to choke. I wasn't sure what I was more worried about, the spray of biscuit all over the table or how red his face was getting.

He'd be able to breathe if he stopped laughing and just swallowed the damned thing, so I didn't feel too bad. "If you choke to death on that, I'm going to put 'Died by dick biscuit' on your headstone." That was evidently funnier than Sawyer's comment, because the laughter flared up again, and even Sawyer finally joined in.

In all the chaos, someone started knocking on the back door. As I got up to check, I heard Melissa's voice over the laughter. "When did you start locking this door?"

Opening it, I gave her a look that said just how stupid that question was. She shrugged and stuck her head in. "They've got clothes on."

"And what if they didn't? Don't just look."

"If they were naked, you wouldn't have opened the door, dumbass. Oh, biscuits! Thanks for dinner."

"I didn't offer." But the words were lost as the boys greeted her, and she started helping herself to the food.

Rolling my eyes, but not caring enough to toss her out, I went back to my seat. Melissa was at the table in seconds, a large bowl of stew in hand as she started to speak again. "Mom said she was going to call you this week. Something about having dinner over at their house next Sunday."

"Anything special?" I couldn't think of anyone's birthday or a holiday I'd missed.

"Um, I think it's pure curiosity." Melissa shrugged and took a bite. "When you mentioned going on a date, it evidently didn't sound casual enough, so she wants to have a chance to grill you. Politely, though."

"Mom's always polite. Just nosy."

Melissa shrugged. "You brought it up."

"Because they're not a secret."

"Then bring them. She'll love the idea that you're finally serious about someone…" She paused and got a faraway look as she poked at her stew. "*Somethem*…? Serious about them…is there a plural of someone? 'Some people' isn't personal enough."

Cooper and Sawyer were watching the exchange like we were an interesting sideshow, but I wasn't sure what was so odd—besides her stupid question. Giving her a "You're being ridiculous" look, I shook my head. "How the hell would I know?"

She shook her head like she was trying to clear out the cobwebs between her ears. "Sorry, I spent all day editing, and it makes you insane after a while."

"So coming over here was just an excuse to get away from your computer. I feel loved."

She pretended to be offended. "Hey, at least I gave you a heads up about the call."

"You have an ulterior motive. I just haven't found it yet." With her, there was always something else going on.

Melissa tried to look innocent, but Cooper laughed. "Your eyes give too much away. That's never going to work."

Melissa glanced over at Cooper and grinned. "How about I take you out to lunch this week, and you show me how, then? I could use some pointers for work."

Cooper gave me a quick glance, but I just gave the tiniest shrug, so he turned back to Melissa and nodded. "Sure."

I wasn't sure if Cooper thought it was a casual offer or

not, but he seemed slightly surprised when she started nailing down a date. "I normally take lunch between one and two, but I have some flexibility if that won't work for you. What days do you have lunchtime off?"

He gave her a wide-eyed look before clearing his throat. "Um, Wednesday?"

It came out more like a question than a statement, but Melissa just charged right past it like his nervousness wasn't an issue. "Great. Do you want me to pick you up, or can you meet me somewhere?"

Still slightly surprised at the direction the conversation had taken, Cooper took a moment to answer. "Um, I work late, so I'll have the car. I can meet you somewhere."

"Great." She took another bite before continuing her interrogation. "When you work late, does Sawyer stay home alone?"

"God, you're so nosy." I rolled my eyes. "Sometimes he and I go out while Cooper is working. Is that what you wanted to know?"

She perked up, nodding. "Yes, I'm thinking about writing a bo—"

"If you finish that sentence, you're a dead woman. I'll tell Mom you turned down a proposal from that accounting geek she loved if you even mention writing a book about my family." I was dead serious, but she just laughed.

Looking slightly impressed she nodded. "That's fighting dirty. All right, I won't mention anything else about it. But that asshole never proposed, and you know it."

"It doesn't matter. Mom loved him and thought he was perfect for you. So she'll keep bringing it up for years, and you know it."

"Cheater."

"If it shuts down that conversation, then absolutely." I

loved her, most of the time, but I was not going to sit back while she wrote a book about our life.

Especially when everything was so new, and Sawyer was still so unsure. My bouncy boy seemed to know exactly how he felt, not that he'd said anything, but I could see the hesitation in Sawyer. There was a fear deep inside that everything that was growing between us would evaporate one day.

I couldn't see the future, but I also couldn't imagine walking away from my sweet boys. I just needed to show him that. He needed to see how serious I was taking the relationship and how much I needed them in my life. It was happening quickly, but I'd never been more sure of what I wanted.

4
_____

COOPER

"This is so sticky, and it just gets everywhere." Cleaning up took forever.

The damned stuff was *everywhere*.

"Then don't wave your hands around next time you've got raw dough on them." Sawyer rolled his eyes and went back to loading the dishwasher.

"It didn't seem like that big of a mess while I was making the biscuits. But this crap is like old cum. It's everywhere and sticky." Balancing on a chair while I cleaned flour and dough off a cabinet door, I ignored Sawyer's groan.

Jackson had cooked, so we'd volunteered to clean up. Well, Sawyer had volunteered us since I'd made such a mess with the biscuits. I hadn't been able to think up a good argument fast enough, though, so I was left wiping down every surface in the kitchen.

"I didn't go on this side of the kitchen. How is there so much flour?"

Sawyer didn't even look at me. "You talk with your hands. We've had this conversation three times in the last five minutes. Just wipe down the flour. I'm almost done, and you keep dawdling."

Because if I took long enough, I was hoping he'd help me. *Duh.*

"It's so hard."

He turned and stuck his tongue out at me. "I'm not doing it. I'm going to go cuddle with Master while you scrape cum off the ceiling."

"Meanie." But I had to laugh because the picture in my head was too weird. "How hard do you think I'd have to orgasm to get cum on the ceiling?"

"Cooper." I could hear Sawyer rolling his eyes.

"What? It's a legitimate question."

"We're not going to try, pup. Got it?" Jackson's voice startled me as it came from behind the chair. His hands grabbed my hips and steadied me. "Why are you up on a chair?"

"Because I'm too short to reach the flour at the top of the doors?" I thought it was obvious.

Jackson shook his head and took the rag from my hands. "Come on. You're never going to finish without killing yourself."

"Hey, you startled me. I was doing fine until you went all stealth to scare me."

"You were staring at the ceiling, not holding on to anything, trying to decide how turned-on you'd have to get before you'd get cum up there. You almost falling was not my fault." Jackson helped me down, giving my ass a smack. "Now, hurry up. Sawyer's right—turtles could go faster."

Then he gave me a suspicious look. "Unless you don't want to cuddle and then get a spanking?" He sighed like it was sad, but he understood. "You just have to tell me if you're not horny and needy and ready to be fucked. There's no need to—"

I stretched up to kiss him. "That's just mean."

"Is it going to get you to go faster?"

Sighing, I nodded. "Yes."

"Wonderful. I'll get the top of the cabinets. You sweep the floor, and then I think that should be all of it." As he started cleaning, Jackson looked over at Sawyer. "Why don't you go get the movie ready? We'll be out there in just a minute."

Sawyer gave him a teasing pout. "How come he gets help with his chores?"

That sounded dirty. Jackson must have had similar thoughts, because his gaze heated, and he started looking at Sawyer like he wanted to do wicked things to him. "How about as a reward for being good, I let you sit on my lap while we watch the movie?"

Jackson's voice dipped lower, and it sent shivers down my spine. I loved it when he went all Dom and dirty. Sawyer started nibbling at his bottom lip but nodded. "Thank you, Master."

I was going to get a spanking tonight, but I had a feeling Sawyer was going to go first. My dick liked that idea too; we both loved watching.

Jackson glanced toward the door. "Go get ready then. I want to be able to hold you and...cuddle you right away. I've waited all day to really...cuddle with you."

I couldn't wait to see what he did to Sawyer while we watched the movie. Those two were like free live 3-D porn when they got going, and Sawyer let his worries fade away. Reaching down to carefully adjust my hardening cock, I felt Jackson's hand smack my ass. "No playing with yourself."

My stupid cock wanted to know what would happen if we didn't listen. But he was a moron, so I kept my mouth shut. I wanted to come and get a spanking, so I was going to behave. "Yes, Master. I'm sorry."

Jackson's hand rubbed slow circles where he'd smacked, and I knew he was thinking about what would happen later. We both were. His rough voice sent shivers down my spine. "My sweet boy clearly needs to be *punished*."

Biting off a moan that wanted to escape. I wasn't sure how to respond. "Please, yes" didn't seem like the best idea. Luckily, I didn't have to say anything because Jackson gave me a nudge. "Sweep."

Nodding, I hurried over to the pantry where the broom was kept. They were right; once I stopped dawdling, it went quickly. In just a matter of minutes, the kitchen was clean, and we were curled up on the couch with the lights down low.

Before Sawyer turned on the movie, I had a few questions that were pushing at my mind. Pressing into Jackson's side, with Sawyer's legs draped over my lap, I leaned my head on Jackson's shoulder. "It was okay that I said I'd have lunch with Melissa, right?"

Jackson had given me the impression that he didn't care one way or the other, but I was starting to second-guess it.

Jackson pressed a kiss to my forehead. "It's fine. If you don't want to, then I'll cancel, but I think she just wants to get to know you guys. It's her way of trying to be your friend and probably just be a nosy-ass that's curious about stuff that's none of her business."

"I don't mind the nosy part. I'm comfortable with who I am and what I like…but she's your sister, and that's…" Serious.

I hadn't dated much, but even I knew hanging out with your boyfriend's family was much more than simply dating behavior. And with us being so much more than just boyfriends, that made it even bigger in my mind.

But how did Jackson feel about it?

"I want you to get to know my family." I heard him kiss Sawyer and then felt another peck on my forehead. "You guys are an important part of my life. I know we haven't been...dating isn't the right word...together long, but this feels right. I'm not going to hide you away. If you want to get to know Melissa, that's fine with me. If the crazy woman scares you, then you can avoid her. My remembering to lock the doors will go a long way with that."

I was still the only person who remembered to lock his doors, so I had to laugh. "Yes, that would help."

The first thing I did when we got to his house was make sure the doors were locked. It had quickly become a habit after seeing how easily Melissa had let herself in. Walking in on dinner was one thing, but when we were playing or getting spanked, that was another. And I did not want to have to stop midscene and check the back door to see if Jackson bolted it.

"Okay, then I think lunch will be fun. I don't have real people in my life besides you guys that I can talk about the puppy stuff with." I had no one I talked about it with besides Sawyer, but that wasn't the point.

"Share what you're comfortable with, but draw clear boundaries if it's something that's none of her business, and you don't want to tell her. Don't feel bad about that." I could hear the concern in Jackson's voice, and it made me smile. He was so cute when he hovered.

"Yes, Sir."

"Good boy."

Sawyer finally spoke. "What about next weekend with your family?"

I felt Jackson shrug. "Well, my mother might want something sit-down, but I was thinking about talking her into barbecuing. I thought something casual might be easier. Steaks or burgers—which do you guys prefer?"

Lifting my head to look at them both, I didn't try to hide my grin. "Um, I don't think that's what he meant." It was cute that Jackson was just thinking about the plans and food, but Sawyer's barely restrained smile said that wasn't what he'd been trying to ask.

"What did you mean, then?" His earnest confusion seemed to relax Sawyer, because he curled into Jackson, smiling.

"Um, I was actually curious if you really wanted us to meet your parents. I know you said us hanging out with Melissa was fine—and by the way, I'm good being left out of that. She makes me nervous—but I wasn't sure if you were ready to tell your parents you were dating two guys."

Jackson's eyes widened as Sawyer spoke, and he started to connect the dots. "I'm planning on you guys being a part of my life for a very long time, baby. I'm not going to hide you. Sure, there'll be times and people that we're more careful with what we say, but not with my family. Now, I don't plan on mentioning the puppy play, because I'm not talking to my mother about my sex life and personal stuff like that, but I can't wait to show them what wonderful people you are."

It was my turn to pop in. "And they're really not going to be upset by the fact that there are two of us?"

Jackson shrugged again. "She's going to be surprised, but she always said she just wanted me happy and settled down with someone. Once she gets past the initial shock, she's going to be fine."

His firm answer, like there was no question in his mind, soothed my nerves, but I could see Sawyer wasn't quite as relaxed. Jackson's parents hadn't lost their shit when he'd come out, and they dealt with Melissa's crazy on a regular basis, so as long as we didn't talk about the puppy play, I figured we might look reasonably normal compared to her.

Jackson gave us both kisses again. "So you'll come with me next weekend?"

"Yes. I'm voting for steaks." I knew Jackson wouldn't bring us into any situation he thought would be upsetting. "You said you were going to show me how to grill."

Sawyer groaned. "You're going to set your hair on fire again."

"What?" Jackson tried to keep his voice calm, but the surprise and worry were clear.

Sighing, I gave his arm a pat. "It wasn't as bad as it sounds. He's just being dramatic."

Sawyer snickered. "You were blowing out birthday candles and set your hair on fire. I have a right to be worried about actual flames."

Jackson's head fell back against the couch. I wasn't sure if I'd lost my chance at barbecuing or not. "You're still going to show me how to do it, right?"

He sighed but lifted his head. "Yes, but with a lot of supervision…*lots of supervision*."

I shrugged. I knew he hadn't been willing to allow me to do it on my own anyway, so it didn't matter that he was planning on hovering. I was going to learn how to grill. "It's going to be fun. I can't wait."

Sawyer and Jackson both looked unsure, but I knew it was for different reasons. Smiling, I tried to show them it would be fine. Being the only non-worrywart was exhausting sometimes.

5

SAWYER

All the discussion of meeting Jackson's family—*and* having lunch with his sister *and* the pending spanking *and* whatever was going to happen—wasn't making it easy to concentrate on the movie.

Jackson's roaming fingers weren't helping either...not that he was trying to be subtle.

When it was just his hand rubbing slow circles on my chest and down to just above my cock, it was slightly distracting, but I wasn't missing much of the movie. But when he got Cooper involved in his scheme, remembering to watch the TV was almost impossible.

His light touch circled around my nipples and then down my chest before starting his invisible track all over again. Each time, he seemed to get closer to my nipples and dick, but he never crossed that line. Finally, on one turn around my nipples, he rubbed the pads of his fingers over the tight tips.

Everything in me tensed, and I waited to see what he would do. Jackson gave a low chuckle and played with the nub, all while watching the movie and talking low with Cooper about stupid things to keep him occupied.

It was distracting as hell.

"Why don't you rub Sawyer's legs? I bet they're tired from such a long day." Jackson's words came out reasonable enough, but one look at Cooper's face showing utter delight and I knew I'd missed something.

"He was very good today, Master." Cooper's sexy innocence made my cock jerk, and Jackson's low sound of approval didn't help either.

"How about we show him how a good boy gets rewarded?"

Sex dripped from Cooper's voice. "Yes, Master."

Fuck.

Somewhere between one explosion and the next, I completely lost what was happening in the movie. Cooper's fingers trailed up and down my legs, caressing in long, slow strokes that kept inching higher.

"He's so tense, Master." Cooper's hands squeezed my thighs, barely an inch from my cock, and it was all I could do to stay still.

"We might need to help him then. He was such a good boy today, and we had so much fun at the park that he needs to be relaxed and happy, doesn't he?" Jackson's idea of helping seemed to include massaging the area right above my cock without actually touching it.

Cooper gave Jackson a very earnest expression and nodded, clearly approving of the direction the conversation was headed. "He's always so good, Master. I want to make him happy."

Fuck.

"Let's see what we can do about that, pup." Jackson's tone almost matched Cooper's with the utter innocence in it, but that illusion was shattered when their fingers started tracing over my cock and balls.

"Oh, Master, he's even harder here. Do you feel all that tension?"

I felt Jackson's body tighten, and I knew he found Cooper's wide-eyed sweetness erotic in a wicked way. Their fingers interlaced over my dick, and I finally had to close my eyes because the image of their hands together over me was too sexy.

Jackson's voice deepened, and I could hear the need starting to grow inside him as well. "You're right. I think we need to see what we can do about this. Are you willing to help me make him better?"

Fuck.

"Yes, Master." Cooper's answer was so earnest it made everything in me tense while I waited to see what they were going to do.

"How do you think we should make him feel better?"

"Should we massage it? That might make it feel better." I could picture Cooper blinking up at Jackson, doing his best to make the naughty idea seem anything but wicked.

"Let's see if that helps. If it doesn't, though, we might need to try something else. When Sawyer's been such a good boy, he shouldn't be this hard and straining." Strong fingers started opening my jeans, and I knew from the large, steady touch that it was Jackson.

"Oh yes, Master. Rubbing his skin is probably much more relaxing." The joy and excitement in Cooper's voice weren't faked, just the erotic artlessness.

They were trying to kill me.

As Jackson freed my dick, their hands wrapped around me, slowly caressing my erection until I was moaning and shaking in Jackson's arms. One hand pulled me tighter to his body while the other kept up the gentle touches that were sending me to the edge.

I wanted to come.

I wanted to beg them to jerk me off harder and let the pleasure explode through me.

But I knew the rules, and I knew the game.

"Why don't you try caressing just the top and see if that makes him more relaxed?" Jackson's words had Cooper moving up my shaft to concentrate on the sensitive head that sent sparks through me with every touch.

The combination was incredible. The tender, steady caress of Jackson's hand and the almost painful pleasure that radiated from Cooper's made it hard to process what was happening. Pain. Pleasure. Soft. Rough. Gentle. Overwhelming.

I was going to come if they kept it up.

Low whines were starting to escape, and I had to clench my jaw down to keep from begging. I wanted so much more, but I didn't want to be in charge.

It was up to Master.

"I think that's working. Sometimes people get tenser right before they relax completely." I wasn't sure if Jackson's words meant that he was going to send me higher before I got to come or not. But I had a sinking feeling it was what the perfectly normal words meant.

"Then we need to make him even harder and stiffer, Master?" I was going to kill Cooper.

Right after I got to orgasm.

"That's probably a good idea." I would never have imagined how hot it would be to lie there and listen to the two of them have such an innocent conversation all while doing such wicked things to me.

Jackson continued the incredible torment and then took it up another level. "Why don't you slide your other hand down between his legs? If you caress him there, it might help us make him even more tense."

"Yes, Master."

Cooper should have gone into acting.

"Lift up for us, Sawyer. We're going to make you feel even better. I know how much you want to relax, my boy." Jackson's words sent waves of need through me, and even though I was stretched out over them, it was almost impossible to get my body to work.

When my pants were down my thighs, I sagged back against Jackson and felt Cooper's hand slide between my legs. Knowing what was coming only made the wait more intense. The seconds dragged out while I felt his finger slip under my balls and over my taint. By the time it was circling my hole, I was shaking and clinging to Jackson's shirt.

"That's a good boy, Cooper. You're doing a great job. Look at how hard you made Sawyer." Jackson's sexy voice brought home the fact that they were watching my every reaction.

"Thank you, Master." Cooper's sweet voice was completely at odds with the naughty thing his finger was doing as it rubbed and teased against my hole. Circling it and caressing over it, he'd press his finger just inside me before pulling it out and starting the maddening circuit again.

As the pleasure continued to build, and I could almost see my orgasm rushing up to crash over me, Jackson's hand stilled. "I think we need to find another way to help Sawyer relax."

"Like what?"

"I'll show you, Cooper." I couldn't decide if I liked the excitement in Jackson's voice or if it made me nervous— probably both. Their hands pulled away from my body, and

I forced my eyes to open. Jackson was smiling at me like he'd thought of the best idea.

Shit.

"Sit up for me, Sawyer. I know just how to make you feel better." My arms, legs, and brain weren't working enough for me to follow Jackson's directions in a timely manner, but with his help, I was soon tucked close to his body while Cooper moved away from us.

"Cooper, I want you to lie down between my legs with your head toward the couch and your feet facing out from it." I was confused as Jackson started stacking the decorative pillows from the couch on the floor between his legs.

When he had Cooper's head propped up on the pillows so his face was right at Jackson's thighs, I was starting to get a naughty picture in my head. Jackson only confirmed it when he started moving me around.

I didn't even think of using my safeword or even denying what I wanted as he laid me out over his lap, so my cock was dangling over Cooper's mouth. Mostly because he didn't ask or make me acknowledge what I wanted.

He just knew and took control.

Maybe I could have eventually admitted what I wanted. Maybe I could have eventually found the words to ask for what I needed so badly: release and the perfect oblivion that came from giving everything up to Master. But I wasn't sure. Thankfully, though, I didn't have to.

"All right, Cooper. As I spank him to get the tension out, I want you to use your lips and give him kisses and take him in your mouth. I think that will help too." Jackson spoke like it was some kind of trial-and-error game he was trying to figure out.

I knew exactly how incredible it was going to feel and exactly how my "tension" would react to their new idea.

As Jackson's hand came down and the heat and sensation spread through me, I sagged over his lap and let everything fade away. When Cooper's tongue finally flicked out and started licking at the head of my cock, I gasped and moaned. The dueling sensations were almost too perfect.

Jackson's hand came down in a soothing rhythm that spread heat across my ass and desire through my body. Somehow the pain of a spanking was never really pain. It was release and surrender and the sparks that sent waves of desire through me.

When Cooper's mouth started sucking at my cock, I was finally able to give up everything. Every worry was gone; every fear faded away. Submission wrapped itself around me like a soothing blanket that took everything that was pressing down on me and pushed it away, leaving just the sensation of being cared for and loved and protected.

As I relaxed into Jackson and mentally offered up my submission, something about the spanking changed. The warmth continued to move through me, and his hand fell down onto me in a steady pattern that let the desire continued to build, but mixed in with the beautiful pain were soothing touches and low murmurs about how sweet I was and how I was so good for him.

Love and desire swirled together in his voice until I couldn't tell them apart, and I wasn't even sure why I'd wanted to in the first place. It was Jackson. He was our lover, our master, our friend…our family.

The pleasure started to swell again, and I wasn't sure I had the strength to hold it back any longer. I wasn't sure if the halting, confusing words that were tumbling out of me let Jackson know I couldn't restrain the pleasure any longer or if he just knew, but he seemed to understand I was at my limit.

His hand stopped spanking me, but the kneading, rough

touch to my tender ass kept the need at an almost impossible level. Jackson said something low as he started teasing circles around my tight hole, but the pounding was so loud in my ears I couldn't hear anything but the roaring of my own pleasure.

Cooper's mouth started working even harder on my cock, and I could finally hear the cries of pleasure that were coming from me. Jackson's spit-slicked finger finally breached my clenched muscles, and the pinch of pain that was mixed with the pleasure was perfect.

As his finger swept over my prostate, sending waves of sensation flooding through me, Cooper swallowed my length down his throat, and all I could feel was my orgasm pushing at me.

"Come."

Jackson's words opened the floodgates, and it crashed over me in absolute perfection. Swirling sensations and pleasure were coursing through me, neither man willing to let me crash back to Earth yet. When it was finally too much, and the raging flood of desire faded, Cooper released my cock and Jackson pulled out of me, rubbing soothing circles on my back.

I heard Cooper move and then felt both their hands caressing me in long strokes down my body. Their words came back into focus slowly.

"So beautiful...look at you..." Jackson's words were low and tender, and I could hear how much it had meant to him.

Cooper was just glad to be right.

His voice was quiet and sweet, but there was an edge of pleasure because he knew he'd been right. "Didn't I tell you how good it would feel? This is exactly what you needed."

I wanted to call him a little brat, but that required more energy than I was willing to find.

When Jackson started turning me in his arms, I groaned. I wasn't ready to move. He chuckled, clearly not put off by my reaction. "Come on. We're going to go lie down in bed. You'll stretch out and relax while I see what I'm going to do to Cooper."

Nodding sleepily as I curled against Jackson's chest, I forced out the words. "Naughty…punish…brat."

Laughing, Jackson ignored my vote and started giving Cooper instructions about pulling my pants and shoes off. When I was naked, he wrapped his arms around me and stood up. I never understood how sexy and how sweet it was to be carried in someone's arms until I'd realized that Jackson could do it.

He laughed and said it was a good incentive for him to keep in shape.

Before long, I was laid out on the bed, my brain finally starting to work but my body making it clear it was done for the night. I felt incredible. I knew I would be stiff, but I just wanted to roll around in the slightly out-of-focus feeling that was wrapped around me and the sensations that were still radiating from my ass.

It was perfect.

6
_____

JACKSON

Cooper's barely restrained excitement almost spilled over as soon as Sawyer was laid out on the bed. He'd been so good, but it was clear his patience was at the end of its rope. Which was perfect because we both wanted me to have an excuse to punish him.

Moving away from the bed and toward Cooper who was waiting in the center of the room, muscles twitching and fidgeting as he stood there, I brought my hands up and started stripping him down methodically.

As his shirt came off, I gave him a serious look. "You were very naughty today, Cooper."

Those sexy, deceptively guileless eyes blinked up at me. "I'm sorry, Master."

God, he was good at that.

It was like he was some sweet little innocent creature that was completely untouched. It was a hot fantasy—one it didn't seem like he was ready to let go of yet. If he wanted to be my naïve boy while I punished him, I would gladly play that game with him.

My hands moved down over his chest and toward his

pants. I wanted my playful boy naked. "You said shocking things to people at the park. You ate candy and begged for more. You even said things to make Sawyer crazy."

As I opened the button on his pants and started sliding the zipper over his erection, I took my time letting my hand caress his cock. "I'm going to have to punish you. It's important that you learn how to be good for your master."

Cooper stared up at me, looking positively crushed that he'd been naughty. If it weren't for his raging erection and the anticipation that was running so high it was making him almost vibrate, I would have completely believed it. "I want to be good for you."

Running my hand along his dick, I nodded slowly before moving my hands to push down his pants. "I'm going to teach you how to be good for me, Cooper."

A low whimper broke through his sexy persona for just a moment before he reined it in. When he spoke, that naughty innocence was back. "Thank you, Master."

When I had him naked, I pulled him into my arms and kissed him gently. Lifting my head, I cupped his face. "I'm going to spank you so next time you think about being naughty, you remember what happens when you misbehave."

It wasn't a question, but Cooper nodded slowly as he shook, and his cock jerked against me. "Up on the bed. I want you stretched out over Sawyer's lap."

The order was clearly not what he'd been imagining, because he cocked his head quizzically before starting to move. As he walked over to the bed, his impossibly hard cock was the only sign of his desire. He honestly looked like an innocent boy who needed to be wickedly punished.

I was clearly a lot dirtier than I'd ever expected, because I was so hard my dick ached at the fantasy laid out before me. Cooper stretched himself over Sawyer's lap, so his hard cock was pressed against Sawyer's soft spent one and he gasped at the pleasure, but it was almost like he was shocked at the naughty position, which made it even hotter.

He was such a wicked influence on me. I was so going to blame the crazy things running through my head on him.

"That's my good boy. Just like that."

He was never going to be able to keep from coming. It was going to be perfect.

Cooper must have realized I wasn't going to make it easy for him to follow the rules, because he gave me a pout as he settled on the bed. Sawyer was still feeling relaxed and lazy, but his hands moved, almost unconsciously caressing Cooper, inadvertently making it even harder for the aroused boy to behave.

I wished I could say that it was all my idea, but this one was all thanks to the internet and dirty books online. It was amazing what you could find when you started looking up book lists with the best gay sex scenes in them.

The book world was an interesting place.

A lot more interesting than I'd realized a month ago.

Cooper watched me intently as I walked over to the nightstand. It was just out of his line of sight, unless he got up and turned around completely, so my surprise wouldn't be ruined quite yet. Setting the lube and condoms on the table, I picked up the last item and tucked my hand against my body.

Climbing onto the bed, I stretched out beside him, careful not to squish a now curious, but still sleepy Sawyer. "What happens to naughty boys, Cooper?"

The hitch in his breath could have been fear, but I knew it was desire. The subtle way he moved over Sawyer's cock gave him away. "They need to be punished, Master."

"That's right. You said you wanted to be my good boy, didn't you?" I waited just long enough to see Cooper nod before I continued. "So, do you know what I need you to ask me?"

He gave me another hesitant nod before shyly looking down and glancing back up through his lashes. "Will you spank me, Master, so I learn my lesson?"

Fuck.

It was hotter than I'd ever imagined.

I was definitely going back and reading *everything* else that author had written.

"Good boy." Finally moving my arm, I brought out the wooden spoon I'd hidden away earlier. Cooper's eyes widened, and he licked his lip.

As I brought the flat of the spoon to rest on one round cheek, I felt shivers racing through him. "I've been doing a lot of research on naughty boys and how to keep them in line. This is supposed to be very effective on willful boys who misbehave."

Before Cooper could respond, I brought the spoon up and down, smacking his ass. I'd explored the idea thoroughly earlier in the week, and aside from feeling a little stupid because I'd been spanking my own ass, I knew I was doing it just hard enough to sting but not actually hurt.

I wanted him frantic and needy, not completely sunk into subspace or in pain.

Cooper arched up and gasped out in surprise but then melted into the bed. Swinging the spoon again, I started peppering his ass with stinging swats that had him writhing against Sawyer. The innocent act fell away as he moaned, and his hard cock thrust against Sawyer's soft body.

All the wiggling and whimpering pulled Sawyer out of his stupor, but he didn't seem to mind. He just let his fingers tease over Cooper's back and down his crack as I spanked him. Cooper was caught between heaven and hell.

He loved being displayed and spanked.

He loved the painful pleasure that was radiating through him.

He wanted more.

He wanted to come.

But he knew begging for more wouldn't get him what he wanted.

I felt Sawyer shift his legs as I rained the spoon down on Cooper's pink bottom, and whatever Sawyer had done sent Cooper into overdrive. One last swat, one last teasing caress over his hole, and Cooper screamed out his pleasure, his orgasm crashing over him.

Keeping it going as long as possible, we teased at his hole and roughly kneaded his tender cheeks while he writhed and shook. When it was finally over, and he was like a rag doll draped across the bed, we changed to slow soothing caresses.

My touch was tender, but the words were heated and rough. "You were a very naughty boy, Cooper. You came without permission during your punishment."

Cooper sighed and pouted, lifting his head to look at me. "Sawyer cheated."

Trying not to laugh, I raised one eyebrow. "How?"

Cooper slumped down again, too tired to hold himself up. "He put my dick between his legs, and it was like I was fucking him. That's cheating."

"I don't see how." Shaking my head, I kept up the gentle sweeps of my hand over his skin. "You were told not to come. You knew the rule, didn't you? We've talked about that before."

He gave me a truly pathetic look that I didn't believe for a second. "No, I'm not going to change my mind. I'm just going to have to think of another punishment for you later."

That had his eyes widening. "Another one, Master?"

"Yes." I sighed like he'd put me in a terrible position, but he didn't seem to believe it. Evidently, I wasn't as good an actor as he was. "I'm just going to have to think of a punishment that fits the naughty behavior I just saw."

Cooper made a little whimpering noise but nodded, clearly curious about what would happen. "I'm sorry, Master."

Flicking my finger over his tight hole, I nodded. "I know you are."

Caressing circles around his sensitive opening, I kept up the teasing as I spoke. "Making sure you understand that you can't be naughty is important. As your master, it's my responsibility to make sure you think about the consequences of your actions."

Easing the tip of one finger into his body, I kept up the sexy words. "Anytime you think about something wicked or naughty, I want you to remember your spanking and your punishment."

Barely fucking him with one finger, I kept going. "You should be thinking about your master when you're a naughty boy."

Cooper moaned and his ass came up, clearly begging for more. I just kept up the maddeningly shallow thrusts while his desire started to stir again. "You're going to think about me, won't you, Cooper? You'll think about me when you're naughty?"

Nodding, clearly not sure what to say, Cooper gave me a needy look. "You said you were going to fuck me, Master. Was I so naughty you don't want to slide your cock into me, Master?"

Fuck.

He was so good at that.

"You've already come, though. You're going to be sensitive, and I won't go easy on you." Easing into him a little more, I knew he felt the stretch by the way his body moved, but his hips thrust back, trying for more, so I wasn't worried.

"Please…you promised…" I wasn't sure if he would come again or not, but the need in Cooper's voice made my cock throb.

My sexy boys had gotten to come, but arousal was still pushing through me.

"As long as you realize that I'm going to fuck you long and hard and that you still have a punishment coming…" I left that part deliberately vague, but I knew exactly what I was going to do with my boy.

He was going to love it.

"Yes…please…" Cooper arched his ass up, moaning as his cock pulled free of Sawyer's thighs.

Sawyer gave me a wicked grin, thoroughly enjoying the way he'd tormented Cooper. Sawyer was cuddly and calm but utterly devious when he wanted to get Cooper back. Life with my boys would never be dull.

Pulling away from Cooper, he whined as I left him empty but sighed in relief when he saw I what I was reaching for. Tossing the lube and condom on the mattress beside Cooper, I slid off the bed and started slowly stripping.

Cooper started to turn for a better view, but I shook my head. "No, I like the view I've got. Your pink ass is tempting and beautiful."

He blushed but looked terribly pleased with himself, which I thought was cute. "That's better. Arch it up for me again. Show me what you want."

Sawyer didn't seem to have any interest in making love with us, but he wasn't going to wait on the sidelines. Reaching for the lube, he slicked up his fingers and eased one into Cooper. The erotic sight had me slowing down so it would last even longer.

Sawyer didn't waste time teasing Cooper. He stretched and readied him until one finger quickly became two, and Cooper was begging for more. Sawyer had a wicked glint in his eyes as he teased Cooper. "You want to feel that stretch as Master sinks his cock in, don't you?"

Cooper's moan must have been a yes to him, because Sawyer nodded and kept talking and playing with Cooper's full ass. "Then you're going to have to wait for more. Look at how hard he is for you. I bet you're so ready. Master made you wait to come for days."

No matter how long I wanted to make the sight last, eventually, I was naked. Climbing up onto the bed, I roughly shoved Cooper's legs apart. As I knelt between them, Sawyer removed his fingers but left his hand resting on Cooper's ass cheek, almost like he was displaying Cooper for me.

"He's ready for you, Master."

Hot. As. Fuck.

"Thank you. I think I'm going to have to find another reward for you." Leaning over Cooper, I kissed Sawyer tenderly. "You're so sweet to think of me."

"I like helping my master." Every time he said the word, it seemed to flow easier from him.

"Thank you, baby." Moving away, I reached for the condom and in seconds had it stretched over my cock.

Sawyer gave me one last bit of help as he played with my cock, smearing the last of the lube over the condom. Fighting back a moan, I gave him a heated look that made him smile and settle back into the pillows. "I think Master's ready for you, Coop."

I was more than ready.

Thrusting into Cooper with one strong push, I loved the

feel of his body clenching around my cock and the moan of pleasure that tore out of him. Sawyer reached under Cooper and another beautiful sound poured out of my needy boy. Guessing that he was playing with Cooper's cock, I started moving in and out with long, slow strokes to send him even higher.

Cooper groaned and begged, pleaded for more and for Sawyer to stop teasing him. Sawyer was going to have to give me a detailed, hands-on explanation about what he was doing to Cooper, but that could wait.

When Cooper started to shake and his desperation to come grew more frantic, I knew we were both at the ends of our ropes. My own orgasm was threatening to burst through me, and I knew I couldn't wait much longer. He felt too good around me, and his pleasure was too beautiful to resist.

Giving Sawyer a nod, I spanked Cooper's ass and growled out the permission he'd wanted to hear for days. "Show me how good it feels. Come for me."

The combination was too much for my worn out, frenzied boy. Cooper exploded, his body gripping my cock almost painfully as the pleasure rode through him in waves. Seeing his passion, I stopped fighting the desire that had been beating down on me.

My orgasm crashed over me, and I kept thrusting into him, wanting to keep us both flying higher and higher. When Cooper finally sagged down onto the bed, I let my softening dick slide out of him. He grunted at the feeling but closed his eyes, letting every muscle go slack as he relaxed.

I moved away just long enough to take care of the condom, throwing it into the trash can by the bed. Climbing back in with them and getting everyone settled was a chore. Cooper had no interest in actually getting off

Sawyer. Sawyer was sleepy and not willing to move enough to shove Cooper off him. Both wanted covers though, and I wasn't going to sleep without my boys wrapped around me.

I won.

Eventually.

When they were finally settled and reasonably clean, Cooper tucked into my side and Sawyer with his head on my chest, they yawned like the sleepy pups they were. Sawyer mumbled low, an exhausted happiness in his voice. "I'm so glad I don't have to get up tomorrow."

Cooper didn't find that nice at all. "That's mean."

"Not my fault you have a morning shift."

"No arguing. You're both exhausted." Giving them kisses as they settled down, I had to smile. They were young, but they were passionate and loving and so cute together that sometimes I wasn't sure how I'd gotten lucky enough to find them.

As sleep fell over us, I heard Sawyer mumble, "I didn't even get to see the movie."

Chuckling, I rubbed slow circles on his back. "We'll watch it again tomorrow."

Cooper huffed and pushed his face into my shoulder. "Without me?"

"You didn't even want to see it." He'd been bored the entire time.

His face scrunched up, and he frowned. "That's not the point."

Smiling, I just shook my head. "That *is* the point, nut. Go to sleep. We'll do something fun later this week when Sawyer has to work."

Grinning like he'd won a huge reward, Cooper finally relaxed. "Yes, Master."

"Cheeky pup." I laughed as Cooper nodded.

"Pup time after work, Master?" Cooper yawned, and I felt Sawyer go still.

"If that's what you want." We had nothing else planned for Sunday, so it would be the perfect time for him to play.

"I want…" Cooper's voice trailed off as he finally fell asleep.

Giving Sawyer another kiss, I pulled him close. "Don't worry. I can hear your brain stirring around. You and I are going to curl up together while he goes crazy for balls and racing around. Maybe you can help me get a surprise ready for him."

"A surprise?" Sawyer's voice wasn't as worried as I'd expected, so I took that to mean we'd made some progress. I just wasn't sure if it was about him showing me his pup, or his accepting that I was fine with waiting until he was ready.

Either way, it didn't matter.

Smiling, I nodded. "Yes. I'll show you tomorrow when he's not around to eavesdrop."

Cooper sighed dramatically. "Meanies."

"Bedtime for pups."

As they finally relaxed, their breathing evening out into slow deep sounds that gave away how tired they really were, I couldn't help but hope Cooper liked his surprise.

7

COOPER

I caught the alarm before it started buzzing a third time, but as I stared at the phone, I couldn't remember setting it. A chuckle came from beside me, and I rolled over in the darkness of the early morning to see Jackson grinning.

"You didn't set the alarm."

"Oh, well. That answers that question." But then I thought of another. "When did you?"

He sighed and stretched, and the sexy expanse of chest was so tempting I brought my hand up and started running my fingers over the muscled plane. Jackson's voice was quiet in the darkness. "I remembered after we fell asleep. Getting untangled from you guys in the middle of the night to go find your phone was a feat, let me tell you."

Laughing softly, I leaned in and pressed a kiss to his lips. "Thank you."

Taking the morning shift on Sunday was terrible, but trading with Mitch had given me Saturday off, so I wasn't going to complain...well, not too much. Jackson rolled over and pulled me close. "You're welcome. Let's get out of here, so we don't wake up Sawyer."

Lifting my head to look over Jackson, I couldn't help but smile as I looked at Sawyer's sleeping form. "Okay. Are you sure you don't want to go back to sleep?"

"No." He leaned in and gave me a quiet, tender kiss. "I think I set it right so you had time to have coffee with me, didn't I?"

Nodding, I couldn't hide my smile. "Yes. You got it perfect."

Even if he hadn't, I would have figured out a way to make it work. I liked the way he did his best to find little bits of time to spend one-on-one with us. And I could tell Sawyer liked it too. When Jackson talked to him about them going out to dinner next week while I worked late, Sawyer had gotten an excited grin on his face and quickly agreed.

It seemed important to Jackson that he get to know both of us as individuals and work on those relationships as well as the one we all had together. I wasn't sure if it was part of the reading and researching he was doing, or if it just seemed like a good idea to him, but we both appreciated it.

No matter if he realized it or not, it made us feel special.

One of Sawyer's fears as we'd started talking about finding a master was that he might like one of us more than the other. Well, that didn't seem to be a problem with Jackson. He liked Sawyer's quiet, steady personality as much as he liked my fabulous excitement.

As we climbed out of the bed, Jackson took a second to make sure Sawyer was tucked in and still sleeping before he moved away. He was so cute, but he had no idea why I was just grinning and watching him. Jackson grabbed a pair of cotton pants that were stacked on the dresser and tossed them to me before getting one for himself.

I bounced through the house once I had clothes on

because coffee sounded delicious, and I couldn't wait to spend a few minutes with Jackson. Of course, I wasn't trying to figure out the best way to discover his secret or what wicked punishment he was planning on torturing me with.

It was going to be wonderful.

Jackson followed at a more reasonable pace, shaking his head and mumbling that it was too early to dance through the house. As I began making coffee and digging out a bagel, Jackson started getting out mugs and yummy things for the coffee.

When we were sitting down at the table with food for me and steaming cups of perfection for both of us, Jackson finally seemed to start actually waking up. "When do you come home?"

It was so cute, but he didn't even seem to realize what he'd said, so I ignored it. "Around lunch. It's a short shift."

He nodded. "All right, then. We'll wait to eat until you get home."

Taking a sip, I thought about the best way to figure out his plans. Scheming helped my brain wake up. "So what's the schedule for the afternoon? Didn't you say you had some errands that we needed to run?"

I already knew the answer to this, but I was curious to see where the conversation would lead. Jackson shook his head and set down his cup. "No, I think I'm good. I know you said you guys needed to buy some groceries before you went back to your place, and I have a little bit of work to do on the books at some point. But there's nothing else that I can think of. I figure we'll just hang out later."

It was good information, but nothing that I could work with.

"Were you and Sawyer going to watch the movie again today?" Maybe that would get things going.

"I think so. It was one he wanted to see, and I kept him…" Jackson grinned, "*distracted*."

That was probably for the best; sitting through it once had been okay because watching Jackson tease Sawyer and then getting to play with him too had been a great distraction. However, watching it twice would be boring.

"Are you going to be able to keep yourself from *distracting* him again?" I had serious doubts about that.

"That's the plan, but we'll have to see what happens." Jackson gave a shrug, and it looked like he wasn't going to try very hard to keep things on track.

"I'm going to guess he'll be pretty frustrated if he has to sit through the movie three times in order to actually see it." Yup, he'd pout at the very least and not the sexy kind.

"Probably, but he didn't seem too frustrated last night, so I'm hoping it won't drive him crazy."

I shrugged as I swallowed my bite of food but shook my head. "Twice is okay, but at three times, he gets frustrated."

Jackson laughed and took another sip of his coffee. "Why do I think you have firsthand experience with that?"

I tried to look casual, but my grin gave it away. "Because you're very smart."

He was still smiling but now looked suspicious. "What did you do?"

Sighing, I drank some of my coffee before answering. "It wasn't that bad."

Jackson gave me a long look. "When your stories start like that, it means it was that bad."

Almost giggling, I nodded conspiratorially. "Well, it was this old movie that was mind-numbing. He kept calling it a classic, and I just couldn't stay interested…or quiet. He said he missed most of it and wanted to watch it again a few days later."

It'd been *terminally* mind-numbing, and I shouldn't have

been held responsible for my actions. "Well...I got bored again. I don't know why actors who've been dead for ages, in movies with terrible action sequences, are considered classics. So to keep from talking...I just found something else to put in my mouth."

Jackson's eyes were dancing, and he was shaking his head. "What did you find?"

"Sawyer's cock." I couldn't help but beam—it'd been brilliant. "It kept me quiet and almost still, but Sawyer got mad because he said he couldn't concentrate while I was sucking him off."

Then I kind of deflated a little and frowned. "For the third time, I had to sit quietly, and he threatened not to throw the ball for me the next time I was a pup if I said a word or moved. It was *sooo* long and *sooo* dull."

Jackson gave me a curious look. "Why didn't he just watch it on a night where you were working late?"

"Clearly to torture me for not shutting up the first time." I was serious, but Jackson snorted his coffee and started coughing.

After a dozen rounds of "Are you okay?" with him just waving me off, he'd caught his breath. "I can see you driving him nuts, but I can't see him not playing with your pup."

I nodded. "Me too, but I wasn't willing to push it. I like playing ball and chasing it when I'm a pup."

His smile turned tender. "I remember."

Nothing that he'd said made it seem like the pup thing was too much, but I asked again, anyway. "And you're okay with me being a pup later...since we're not going anywhere?"

"Of course." He answered without even thinking about it.

Finally breaking down, I asked about my reward. "Am I going to get my surprise later?"

Laughing, Jackson reached over and ran a hand down my face. "I'm shocked it took you this long to ask."

He was sweet, but that wasn't the answer I was looking for. Sighing, I gave him a pout. "I tried hinting, but you wouldn't tell me."

My cuteness didn't work. He shook his head. "Because it's supposed to be a surprise."

Putting my elbows on the table, I rested my head in my hands and gave him my best sad puppy dog look. "But that's no fun."

"It is for me." Jackson grinned and pointed to my food. "Now, eat your breakfast. If you hurry, we have time to get a shower together if that's what you want."

Oh, yes.

Nodding enthusiastically since I had a mouthful of coffee, I tried to let him know that was exactly what I wanted.

Jackson chuckled. "All right, I'm going to grab a few things and take them to the guest bathroom, so we don't wake Sawyer. You finish up, and I'll see you in there in just a minute. Sound good?"

"Sounds perfect." And if he was worried about us being loud, I was pretty sure that meant we were going to have some fun.

"Good." He rose and leaned over, giving me a quick peck. "Don't dawdle."

"I don't think that will be a problem." Cramming in another bite of the bagel while he started walking out, I was finished with breakfast in a matter of minutes. It took a little bit longer to make sure everything was clean and put away before going to meet him, but I didn't want to leave him a mess.

As I headed into the guest room, I saw a pile of clothes on the bed, and I heard Jackson moving around in the bathroom. He was just turning the water to the shower on as I walked in. His sexy body and thickening cock were a beautiful distraction, so it took me a moment to realize I was supposed to be getting naked too.

Giving me a heated look, Jackson let one hand slide down his body and start caressing his dick. Not exactly trying to get it hard, but clearly playing with it for my benefit. I wasn't sure if the sexy sight made me go faster or slower. I wanted to feel him wet and pressed up against me, but I also wanted to watch his hand as it moved.

When I was finally naked, my cock was painfully erect. Jackson's wandering hands made me even harder as he helped me into the shower. It was smaller than the one in the master bathroom, but there was enough room for both of us, especially if we stayed close.

As Jackson started rubbing the body wash slowly over me, he began taunting me. "You're going to have fun this afternoon. I'll have your surprise ready for you, and then you get to be a pup for me."

The feel of his hands caressing slowly over me, and his sexy voice teasing me had me squirming and pressing my ass up against his cock. I wanted to feel his dick sliding into me and fucking me senseless.

"No, my boy, not that. You still have to be sore from last night."

I could feel it, but it wasn't bad. "But—"

"You're going to have your tail later, and I don't want that to be too much for you. But if you want to come, I might be willing to wrap my hands around your cock. Do you want my fingers teasing your balls and my hand rubbing along your shaft while the water beats down on you?" Jackson's husky voice sent a shiver down my spine, and a whine escaped.

One hand slowly started moving down my abs toward my cock, and the other started working its way from my hip to my chest. By the time he was actually playing with me, I was so ready I was shaking. As his hand slowly started going up and down my shaft and his fingers started plucking at my nipples, I mentally cheered his decision for us to use the guest bathroom.

Moans and cries of pleasure as he teased at the head of my dick or pinched a sensitive nub echoed through the room, and I had to fight to keep them in. Jackson's head came down, and he whispered low as he kissed my ear.

"My loud boy, I love hearing your sounds, but if you wake up Sawyer, I'm going to have to think up another punishment. You already have one waiting for you—don't make it two." Biting my lip as he continued to methodically push me closer to the edge, I whimpered and made low begging noises that I hoped were quiet enough.

But the threat of another punishment made it almost impossible.

The ideas running through my head were so tempting and so incredible. Just the idea of what he might do was enough to have me thrusting my cock harder into his hand.

"Does my boy want to come? Are you ready to show me how good it feels?" Jackson's thumb ran over the head, and he pressed gently down on my slit making waves of pleasure run through me.

"Please...yes..." I would have kept begging, but Jackson knew that he couldn't tease me for too long.

I wasn't sure if that was a good thing or not.

I loved the way he kept pushing me higher. I loved the way he wanted to see how much pleasure he could send rushing through me. But the thing I loved most was when he growled out the words I was always desperate to hear.

"Come, my sexy boy."

I was too loud. I knew it. But as my orgasm crashed over me, all I could do was shake and give everything over to Jackson. Cum shot out in long ropes onto the floor as the pleasure rolled through me. He kept up the sexy torture until I sagged back into his arms.

While I fought the urge to just sink into him and simply enjoy the water beating down on me as I cuddled into him, Jackson continued washing me off. "Come on, pup. You have to work."

"Work sucks." Sticking my head under the spray to chase the fog away, I reached for the shampoo and finished getting ready.

When we were both done, he turned off the water, and we started drying. I must have been a cat in another life because I was filled with more curiosity than common sense. "What's my punishment going to be, Master?"

I just had to know.

Jackson's smile, which had been simply cheerful as we'd gotten out of the shower, took a wicked turn. I wasn't sure if his pleased-with-himself expression was a good thing for me or not. He took a step closer and cupped my cheek. The tender touch clashed with the wicked look in his eyes.

"If I tell you now, then that will be when the punishment begins. Do you understand that?"

Oh.

Work. I had to work. My brain was caught between thinking about my responsibilities and saying, *Fuck it, I don't care.* "Um, can I ask a question first?"

His thumb traced my cheek, and his smile turned slightly sweeter. "Of course."

"I'll be able to go to work and function?" I wasn't sure

what he had in mind, but some things that had run through my head would have left me too turned-on to think, much less work.

"I can guarantee you'll be able to work." Then he thought for a moment. "And you might even work more efficiently, from what I saw online."

His research was going to kill me.

Really only days into our relationship and he was trying to be the best master he could for us. "Okay then, Master. I want to know."

My stomach whirled in anticipation as Jackson quietly watched me. When he started to reach down and cup my dick, I was a little confused. Then he started to explain. "I have a cock cage that's going to keep you nice and soft, locked away for me."

What?

I could feel my eyes widen, and the look on my face made Jackson grin. "You're not going to be able to get hard without permission. I think that's a fair punishment for coming when you were told not to."

He hadn't asked my opinion, and it wasn't a question, but I found myself nodding. It was...perfect.

"Good boy. If you behave, then I'll only leave it on for a couple of days."

"Days?" I finally found my voice, but it came out louder than I'd intended.

"Yes." His calm answer wasn't enough information, but my brain was having a hard time putting everything together.

I wasn't going to play innocent and claim I didn't know what he was talking about. I'd watched enough porn and had read enough fun stuff on the internet to be able to picture exactly what he wanted to do, but it was still...sexy and a little insane.

"How many days? Do I get to…well, come isn't the right word, but I don't—" My brain wasn't working enough to figure out what I needed to say.

"I haven't decided how many days yet, pup, and yes, I plan on touching you and kissing you and making love to you and absolutely torturing you with pleasure."

"But my dick won't get hard?"

"That's correct."

"You're a wicked master."

He gave me a tender kiss. "I know. Now finish drying off and go lie down on the bed. I want to get you ready, so you're not late for work."

Work. *Fuck.*

"But I can't—"

Jackson interrupted. "It's designed for long-term wear, so it should be comfortable. I'm going to leave it unlocked just in case it needs to come off, because I know I can trust you to leave it on. And before you mention the bathroom or anything like that, I looked up your store online and you have the small, individual rooms instead of big bathrooms, so it will be fine."

"But I'm going to be so turned-on." That came out whiny, but when he reached for my towel I handed it over and started walking toward the bed.

"Yes, you are, and I can't wait to see how sexy you look." Jackson's words stunned me as I sat down on the edge of the bed by the pile of clothes that wasn't looking so innocent anymore.

"You think it's sexy?" It was already interesting and erotic in a curious way, but when Jackson nodded and gave me a heated look, that took it to a whole new level.

As he started to speak, I lay back on the mattress unselfconsciously. His sensual words made my cock jerk, and I was grateful he'd already let me come. "I think that seeing you run around chasing after the ball, with your tail wagging and your dick soft and locked away, is going to be one of the sexiest things I've ever seen."

"Oh…" I hadn't really thought about the puppy play with the cock cage on.

How was I supposed to work with all this running through my head?

"But if it's too hard and too distracting?" I looked up at him, worried about disappointing him but wanting to obey.

Jackson leaned over me and gave me a kiss. "Then you won't wear it for work, but you will wear it here and at the apartment. Does that make you feel better?"

Nodding, I took a deep breath. "And you won't be disappointed?"

"No, baby, but I think it's going to be fine. I've done a lot of reading on it, and there are plenty of guys who go to work every day locked away by their partners and Doms." He said it like there was nothing strange about that sentence.

As he straightened and reached under the clothes, he brought out the cage. It was plastic, and I'd seen other ones like it before, so I knew he was right; it was one for long-term wear. And the fact that I knew that said I'd watched entirely too much porn over the years.

In minutes—probably less—my cock was restrained, and I was dressed. Jackson had picked out my loosest black pants to go with my uniform shirt and for that, I was grateful. Looking down, it was completely unnoticeable, but it was still weird.

Sawyer came in just as I was ready to walk out the door. Mumbling sleepily, he gave both of us strange looks. "You guys look like you're up to something. Cooper, what did you do? It's too early for crazy."

Laughing, Jackson walked over and pulled him in for a

hug. "He found out about his punishment for coming when he wasn't supposed to."

Some of the fog faded from Sawyer's face, and he looked me over, clearly expecting to see something out of the ordinary. "What is it?"

Grinning like a very pleased master, Jackson didn't try to hide how excited he was. "Come here, Cooper, so we can show Sawyer. I think he's going to like it."

Caught between finding the whole thing hot and still a bit confusing, I walked over. Jackson wrapped his other arm around me and gave me a kiss. "Unzip your pants so he can see."

If it hadn't been physically impossible, the order would have made my dick hard. As it was, it just stirred things low in my body and made me want to whine. "Yes, Master."

I saw a shiver race through Sawyer at the words, and I had to smile. I'd already come, but he was waking up horny, and we were only making it worse. As I opened my pants and pushed down the tight briefs I was wearing, the cage became visible.

"*Fuck.*" Sawyer's low expletive was filled with shocked arousal.

"I know, right?" It was hot.

His hand came out and gently caressed the plastic that encased my cock. "That's so cool."

He wanted it too. I could see it in his eyes. "This is how Master said I had to be punished for coming when I wasn't supposed to." I let the sexy words sink into his brain before I continued. "I think it's probably going to be the same punishment for you...if you're naughty."

Eyes widening, Sawyer looked to Jackson who was nodding and watching every reaction Sawyer made. He clearly wasn't missing the interest that was rolling off

Sawyer in waves. "Yes, I think it's a reasonable consequence for your actions."

We both nodded, although Sawyer was clearly still in shock.

As much as I wanted to stay and tempt Sawyer, I had to go. Leaning close to both of my men, I gave them quick kisses. "I have to go, but I'll see you after work. Have fun."

"Oh, we will." Jackson's words made my cock try to harden and the weird sensation had a whimper escaping.

It was going to be a long day...a long couple of days.

8

SAWYER

"That was good." Stretching and sitting up, I smiled at Jackson.

"So you're glad I behaved myself this time?" One eyebrow went up, and he gave me a teasing grin. "I got a lecture from Cooper this morning that you might not mind it if I distracted you once, but I should be very careful about doing it a second time."

Laughing, I leaned back into him again. "He was nuts, but the blowjob was great. I had to watch that movie three times—that's just ridiculous."

Jackson's arms wrapped around me, and I could feel him chuckling. "He just wanted to make sure I understood there were consequences for my actions."

"I'm glad he warned you. I appreciate your restraint, but I think the fact that we stayed in bed most of the morning helped too." After Cooper had left for work, we'd gone back to bed and he'd made love to me. We'd cuddled and slept more before finally getting up and making breakfast.

It had taken us so long to actually function for the day that by the time we'd started the movie, we didn't have that much time to wait until Cooper came home. *Home.* I was starting to do it too. Jackson's habit of calling it our home too was making it hard to keep my distance.

Jackson's phone chimed again, and we both groaned. I sat up as he reached for it off the coffee table. I knew who it was going to be, and I wasn't sure if it was funny or frustrating. "If it's another dick pic, we're going to have to do something about that."

Laughing, Jackson held up a picture of Cooper's trapped cock. It looked like he was sitting in his car taking the picture, angling it down at his lap. Jackson thought he was cute. "He's just excited."

I rolled my eyes and flopped back against the couch while he typed a response to Cooper. "He's going to get arrested."

Jackson chuckled. "He said he put his toy away." Setting the phone back down, Jackson smiled at me. "And he said that he and his toy are on their way home. He also said that his cock wasn't sure if it liked being in the cage."

"Of course he did." The little ham had been texting indecent things all morning.

We'd woken up to find three pictures of his dick that he'd taken in the bathroom mirror. They'd been accompanied by messages that went from whining about being horny to wanting to know if it looked cute locked away.

Little attention whore.

Jackson wrapped his arms around me and lay back against the arm of the couch, pulling me so I was stretched out over him. His hands slid down to cup my ass, and he shifted me so our cocks were rubbing against each other. "I think you are just a little jealous. I saw how you looked at his cage this morning."

I'd kind of hoped we weren't going to talk about that.

However, considering the number of other things he didn't make me talk about, this one wasn't the worst he could have brought up. Taking a deep breath, I curled into him, resting my head on his shoulder. "Maybe?"

His fingers started to knead the muscles of my ass, and it was distracting enough that I almost missed his next words. "Just maybe? I saw the way you touched it, and the way you let your fingers trail over the smooth cage. Did you want to know how it would feel?"

"Yes." Simple questions that didn't require actual sentences were so much easier when the topic was slightly embarrassing.

"Do you like the idea of not only giving me control of your orgasms but your ability to get hard as well?" Before I could answer, Jackson continued, his husky voice sending a shiver through me. "Now, I probably shouldn't try to influence you, but I have to tell you how erotic I find it."

Denying the truth would have been even more wrong since he'd been honest. "Yes."

"Before you go back to the apartment, do you want me to put a cage on you? Not because you've been naughty, but so you can remember who you belong to? Should I make sure my boys leave with matching cages keeping their cocks nice and soft and ready for me to let them out?" Jackson made no effort to hide how the fantasy affected him. His hard dick rubbed against mine as he used his grip on my ass to shift me back and forth over him.

Fuck.

"I…" I wasn't sure what to say.

Did I like the idea of being locked away for him?

73

Yes.

Would it be hot to know that he really wasn't going to let us come?

Yes.

Had I liked the way Cooper had looked in it?

Hell, yes.

Was I ready to ask for it?

Probably not.

"Yes." It didn't come out as confidently as I wanted, but just the fact that I was admitting it was a big step.

Jackson pressed a kiss to my cheek but didn't make a big deal out of it, which I appreciated. "Then that's what we're going to do. Once we figure out if you guys are staying the night or heading back to the apartment, we'll iron out the details. But basically, I'm just going to put it on right before you leave."

Nodding, I tried not to let the images run rampant in my head. Needing a distraction, I lifted my head to be able to look at Jackson. "You said something to Cooper about a surprise? If he's going to be home soon, then do we need to get something ready?"

Jackson looked like a kid who had a juicy secret. "Yes, but we're going to have to hurry. Come on."

Giving my ass a pat, he urged us off the couch. Glancing down, he shook his head. "We need clothes."

Well, whatever we were doing involved leaving the house, because evidently sleep pants weren't enough clothing. Jackson refused to say exactly what we were doing as we hurriedly got dressed. When we were ready, I expected him to take us out front to the cars, but instead, he started walking us over toward the other side of the property where the training building was.

Rolling my eyes, I finally gave in and started asking

more questions. "What are we doing? He's going to be here in just a few minutes."

Jackson grinned. "We're going to set up an obstacle course in the living room for Cooper's pup."

What?

"Ohh."

"Just a few things this time, but eventually, I'm going to figure out how to make it work out here. Right now, I don't like the fact that he'd be on concrete, and it's not as clean as I'd want for him. But I think the house will be fine."

Cooper was going to get to run through an obstacle course.

I was a cuddly pup, maybe even slightly lazy, so running over things and basically doing tricks didn't really sound appealing, but I knew Cooper would love it. If I was jealous of anything, it was that Cooper was so confident and had such a good time showing Jackson his pup side.

The idea didn't give me hives anymore, so I thought I was making progress.

Jackson seemed to know what I was thinking, or at least some of it, because he shook his head. "At your own pace, Sawyer."

Reaching out to take his hand, I gave it a squeeze. "I know."

"So, you think he's going to like it?" There was a hint of nervousness behind the words that was sweet, and it showed how much he was thinking of Cooper...both of us, really.

"He's going to love it. He's going to be bouncing off the walls." I smiled as Jackson relaxed and started walking even faster.

The first thing that Cooper had packed for our weekend with Jackson was his puppy gear—and mine as well. He'd made it very clear that it was just in case and promised not to bring it up to Jackson. Cooper was going to love getting to play with more than just balls and rope toys.

As Jackson led me into the large open space, I couldn't help but picture Cooper chasing balls and playing in all the space. It was amazing. But yes, with the concrete floors and the openness it was cool and probably not someplace he needed to be crawling around. But there was potential.

"Maybe an area where some of those foam mats can go to cushion the floor?" Jackson had the almost warehouse-style building divided into different areas. Some were just ropes that acted as fencing so the spaces could be opened up, but others had small walls that neatly marked the divide.

Jackson nodded and pointed toward the back. "I was thinking about using one of those penned off areas. Something like those black exercise mats to make it easier to crawl on would be perfect."

"I agree—and a bit more privacy as well."

He chuckled. "Yeah, I think I'd need new locks and something better covering those windows just to be sure."

I had to agree. "Cooper would not appreciate your sister walking in on him like that." And neither would I.

"No, locks and coverings would be the first thing to consider. But for now, the stuff I was thinking about is over there." He walked over to a long cabinet and started pulling out what looked like oversized building blocks, but I quickly realized what they were: little fences.

"He can jump over these for today, and I have...there it is...a tunnel that he'll fit through. Just grab a few things you think he'd like." Jackson was excited as we pulled out the toys he thought Cooper would enjoy.

He glanced over when I didn't move. "They're clean, so you don't have to worry. I wouldn't have suggested—"

Smiling, I shook my head and interrupted his OCD

explanation of how clean it was. "No, that's not it. I was just...surprised at how much thought you've put into all this. I know we haven't really...been around that long and it's..."

I was feeling stupid, and I wasn't sure how to explain it.

Jackson leaned in and gave me a tender kiss. "It's happening fast, and you just don't see how it works as well as it does?"

Nodding, I tried not to look away. "Yes, basically."

He gave me a tender smile. "It doesn't feel that fast to me most of the time. When I got that first email, it was like a lightbulb went off inside of me, and it just kept pushing me to find out more. It kept pushing me to you. Nothing you guys have told me or shared scares me. I like not only how different you both are, but how honest and sincere and strong you are as well."

With one last tender kiss, he pulled away. "Let's get this back to the house and set it up." Then his I've-got-a-secret smile broke out again. "There's something else in the house I want to show you."

Cooper and I might be young, but Jackson was the biggest kid of all.

As we made it back to the house with our loot from his business, Jackson started getting even more excited. He forced himself to focus on the living room, moving the coffee table out of the way and setting up the little obstacle course he'd envisioned before moving on to his last surprise.

When we were down to seconds before Cooper would be walking in the door, Jackson grinned. "Come on, the last part is in the guest room."

I'd been in there earlier, and I couldn't remember anything out of the ordinary in the room. "What is it?"

"I went out and got them the other day. I wasn't sure if I should wait to get them out or not, but I'm not sure there's a reason to wait. It's not like either of you have to use it until you're ready. It'll wait." It was more information than when I'd started asking questions, but Jackson didn't seem to realize the answer was not sufficient.

"But what is it?" If it would wait until we were ready, then I was guessing it wasn't food. There was always the chance it was more toys, but that wasn't what I was picturing.

His eyes danced. "I think you've already guessed."

Possibly.

My nerves were slightly on edge as he walked over to the closet, which probably made me the biggest wuss ever. As Jackson opened it, he stepped back in an almost ta-da fashion. Yup, he was my big kid, all right.

"Aren't they perfect? Feel. They're so soft." It was like it was Christmas morning for Jackson.

Puppy beds.

Crossing the last few feet to stand beside him, they weren't as overwhelming as I'd expected. They basically looked like two oversized pillows, just with slightly raised sides and tags that said how perfect they would be for a large-breed dog.

I think we qualified as large breeds.

Reaching out to touch them as Jackson wrapped himself around me, I couldn't help but think of how they would feel against my skin. One blue and one brown, they were soft— like a blanket that you just wanted to curl up in on cold nights. As I moved my hand over it, I felt the padding underneath, and I knew it would be comfortable to lie on.

"It feels nice." Not my most descriptive sentence, but I hadn't just stood there staring, so I was pretty pleased.

"They have a memory foam core that makes it really comfortable. The lady in the store thought I was crazy for sitting on it, but I wanted to make sure it was comfortable enough for you both." Jackson pulled me tighter against him and pressed a kiss to my cheek. "There is no rush, remember? I just wanted you to have one too. You're both very important to me."

He'd tried out dog beds for us.

Leaning back in his arms, I closed my eyes to relax for just a moment. I finally smiled. "How many beds did you sit on before you picked these out?"

Jackson laughed. "About ten at three different pet stores. You weren't supposed to ask that."

Taking my hand off the pillow I turned in his arms. "Thank you. Let's get these set up before Cooper gets home."

Grinning like a kid, Jackson nodded. "He's going to love it."

He was right. Cooper was going to be over-the-moon excited.

Dragging out the beds and getting them set up in the living room took no time at all. Placing them in a corner just off to the side of the couch, they looked like regular puppy beds. Curling up on the couch with Jackson to wait for Cooper, I looked over at them. "Are you going to keep them out all the time?"

Jackson shrugged. "Most of the time. I know you don't want to share that part of yourself with just anyone, so we can easily pick them up and put them away if we have company or someone in the family is coming over. We can say that I was watching a friend's dogs while they were out of town if we can't put them in the closet before they come in."

Nodding, I knew he was right, but the idea of having them out felt weird. In the time that we'd known him, his sister was the only one who dropped by—he was more of a homebody than we were—but it was still...odd.

"It's going to take some getting used to." I thought it was a subtle way of saying how strange it was, but Jackson just started chuckling and wrapped his arms tighter around me.

"Somehow, I thought you would say that." There was no malice in his voice, and it was clear that he didn't mind at all. I shook my head and ignored his teasing.

"When do you think Coop—"

Before I could even finish the sentence, I heard Cooper bounce through the front door. "I'm home, but you two need to start locking the door. I cannot be the only person who remembers to do that."

As he walked into the living room, he stopped and his mouth fell open. "Ohhh..."

Jackson stilled, and I sat up, giving him one last kiss, so he could stand and go over to Cooper. Curling up on the couch, I watched as Jackson slowly made his way to Cooper, then wrapped his stunned boyfriend in his arms. They were both so funny.

"Oh, Master...it's...and it's a...you..." And the nut was finally speechless.

All it took was ridiculously priced dog beds and an obstacle course.

"What do you think?" Jackson tried to sound calm, but I could hear the nervousness in his voice.

He was the sexiest Dom in bed and loved to push us to the limit and make us crazy, but other times he was sweet and tender—and worried about pleasing his pups.

"It's amazing." Cooper's wide-eyed stare never moved from the perfection that was laid out in front of him. "Thank you, Master. Can I be a pup now? Can I play?"

Jackson gave Cooper a slightly indulgent, but no less

pleased with himself, smile and nodded. "Yes. Let's get you ready."

In minutes, a decked-out pup was dashing around the living room, only pausing when the cock cage occasionally startled him. I gave the two of them time to kiss and cuddle as Jackson got him ready, but once Cooper had his knee pads and mitts on, he'd given his tail a wag and barked before running around at top speed.

Through the tunnel and over the jumps, he barreled through the living room as fast as he could go. Jackson would laugh when Cooper's cock would try to harden, causing him to give a little whine. The fact that he would then shake his tail to try to get turned-on, which only started the whole cycle over again, had neither of us feeling bad for him.

Cooper liked being denied even when he wanted to come.

It made me wonder what it would look like on me and how it would feel. I wasn't going to be the type to send selfies of my trapped cock to Jackson all day long, but it was going to be incredibly erotic.

If just being told we had to ask for permission to come was hot, being denied access to even getting erections would be even hotter.

As Jackson settled down on the floor, out of the way of Cooper's mad race, he glanced over at me and smiled. "Come cuddle with me. Eventually, he's going to get bored and want us to throw the ball."

I smiled as I stood and started walking over to him. "I don't know about that. He's gone through that tunnel a dozen times already."

Cooper's pup needed lots of stimulation and excitement, and Jackson's idea had been perfect. Dodging an excited pup who burst out of the tunnel barking, I laughed and made my way across the room. Giving the blue bed a long look, I took a deep breath and made a small detour.

Carrying the cushion closer to him, while he pretended not to pay attention to what I was doing, I lay down and curled up on it, resting my head on his lap. Jackson's hand came up and started running through my hair and down my back.

It was almost perfect.

The bed was soft, and Jackson's touch was tender and soothing. I knew it would feel even better when I was a pup, but it still seemed so hard. Jackson didn't seem to mind as I moved even closer to him, almost as a pup, but not completely.

He didn't ask questions or make me speak, but he didn't seem to expect me to act like a pup either. He was content with the half step I'd taken and honestly seemed to simply enjoy cuddling with me while Cooper played and barked.

Watching Cooper come flying out of the tunnel, that time with his ball in his mouth, I smiled as he stopped in front of Jackson. Dropping his chest low, he arched his tail up and started wagging it. A low whimper escaped as he let the ball fall to the floor.

He didn't stop wagging his tail, though.

Jackson didn't seem to have any pity for the poor, horny pup. If anything, Cooper's frustration turned him on. It was kind of hot to watch.

"You're being punished, pup." Jackson reached out and ran his hand over Cooper's head. "No erections for you, but you can show me how you wag your tail. I bet that feels good, doesn't it?"

Confusing sensations seemed to be running through Cooper, and I couldn't wait to ask him about it later. The trapped feeling of being owned seemed to clash with the fabulous way the plug rubbed against his prostate, because he'd wag and whine and then wag again.

I was a little jealous, but not enough to go get my tail out. Not yet, at least.

"That's my pretty pup. Wag it faster." Jackson's hand reached down to start rubbing along Cooper's back and Cooper turned, trying to beg for more.

Jackson chuckled but let his hand slide along Cooper's side to rub his belly. Skipping over his dick, Jackson caressed Cooper's balls before reaching through his legs to nudge the plug. Somehow, watching his hand going through Cooper's legs like that was even hotter.

Cooper moaned at the pleasure that seemed to course through him. Jackson chuckled again before reaching down to grab the ball. Throwing it across the room, he gave Cooper a smile. "Go fetch, pup."

Jackson's hand came down to rub my head as Cooper ran over to the ball, only to get distracted by the tunnel again. Smiling, I closed my eyes and soaked up the warmth of Jackson's touch and the sound of Cooper playing.

When Cooper finally remembered to bring the ball back, I felt Jackson move. I knew Cooper was getting more teasing caresses from the way he whined and the little needy bark that escaped.

"Some pups can come just by wagging their tail, even when they're locked away like you are. We'll have to see if we can teach you. Would you like that? Would you like to feel how good it is to have all that pleasure rush through you when your dick is still locked away?" Jackson didn't seem to need an answer, even though Cooper's bark was clearly an agreement. "I think you would."

I heard the sound of the ball thudding across the room, and Jackson's hand came back down to start rubbing long strokes down my back. The warmth of his body and the softness of the bed had me relaxing even further. As I finally started to drift off, I heard Jackson speaking quietly. "My pretty pup."

I had a feeling he wasn't talking about Cooper—and for the first time, there was no fear and no worry when I thought of showing him the quiet part of myself that I kept hidden away. Master thought I was perfect just the way I was.

9

JACKSON

Throwing myself onto the couch, I looked at my phone and gave myself a mental pep talk. I wasn't exactly nervous, but it was a big deal, and I felt the weight pressing down on me. Swiping my finger across the screen, I quickly brought my mother's number up and let the call connect.

When she finally picked up, I could hear the smile in her voice. "Jackson, I thought I was going to get a call from you."

The not-so-subtle guilt trip hit its mark. "Sorry, it's been a little busy the past couple of days."

Try a busy couple of weeks.

Between work and the time I was spending with my boys, calling friends and even family had been bumped down the to-do list. Which was probably why Melissa didn't even bother calling and just showed up randomly.

"Melissa said you'd been busy. How is work going?" Her voice was even and nothing about it said she knew more than I'd already told her. I was glad Melissa had kept her mouth shut.

"It's going great. Classes are full, and everything's going

very well." And now to the real reason I called. No point in putting it off because then it would sound like I was ashamed of them. "Do you remember when I told you that I had a date a few weeks ago?"

She paused for a moment. "Yes, someone you met online, correct?"

"Yes." She'd learned to give us some space as we'd gotten older and had started answering her questions honestly, so it wasn't that surprising when she didn't press for details immediately. "Well, I've been seeing them for a while, and I'd like to bring them over on Sunday for dinner."

She was quiet for several long seconds, so long it was starting to make me nervous. "Them? That's another pronoun for—what did they call it the other day on the radio? Gender something or non-something...before you bring them over, your father and I need more information, sweetie. I don't think I know how to use 'them' in place of he or she without offending someone. Can I say 'someone,' or is that wrong? I don't remember."

My head fell back against the couch. "Thanks for being so open-minded, but, um, no, it's actually two guys that I'm seeing...them...the two of them."

"Oh." The long pauses were going to get on my nerves.

Finally, she started talking again. "Is bringing them both over at the same time a good idea? I know that dating around is common. Lydia down the street said her daughter is seeing a man and a woman, right now. We would love to meet the men you're dating, but I don't want drama—"

"I'm not dating two guys at the same time." So that wasn't exactly right. "Well, I am but not like that. They're already a couple, and we're all dating together."

"Ohhh." Another long pause had me fidgeting and reaching for the remote. Turning on the TV and muting it, I started flicking channels. When she found her words, I kind of wished she'd kept them to herself. "It's like the sixties all over again."

"*Mother.*"

She laughed. "You're such a prude."

"I'm private."

"If that's what they're calling it these days, that's fine." She chuckled again. "Now, tell me about your gentlemen friends."

"They're great. Sawyer works for a landscaping developer and helps put together the plans for large corporate jobs, and Cooper is a barista, but he's going back to school because he's up for a managerial position and might be running his own store soon." Trying to think of what else wouldn't be oversharing, I kept going. "Cooper is funny and outgoing. Sawyer is definitely quieter and more laid-back."

"They sound very nice. Going back to school can be hard. Is Cooper changing careers? One of those boys down the street that you used to hang out with in high school recently did that. His mother was saying he started out with an English degree, but now he's going back to school to be an accountant. It's been tough. He's been complaining that the age difference between him and his classmates is significant. She thinks he should switch to a strictly online program, but—"

Knowing her tendency to keep going, and not seeing an end in sight, I jumped in. "Cooper isn't that much older than everyone else in the program."

And three…two…one…

"How much younger than you is he, Jackson?"

Me dating two guys or the non-binary individual she was picturing was fine, but me dating a younger man was scandalous, evidently. "Lots."

"Jackson." I could almost hear her shaking her head.

"They don't mind the age difference, and it doesn't feel that significant most of the time." So, maybe I was lying, but I wasn't going to explain that they liked having a master who was older.

That could jump from oversharing to just plain weird.

"Did you find them on one of those sex apps? Jackson, I—"

Laughing so hard I almost fell off the couch, it took me a minute to be able to respond, but at least it stopped the crazy train she was on. "No, I didn't find them on some kind of hook-up app. They're nice guys and looking for something serious. I promise. You're going to love them."

And it was time to play the ace in the hole. "Their own families basically disowned them a few years ago when they came out. They're nervous about meeting you guys."

She switched from worried I'd been stalking twinks on sex apps to overprotective mother hen mode in seconds. "Oh, Jackson, that's terrible."

"They didn't really believe me when I said you weren't going to care that there are two of them. They're prepared for the worst." The fact that I didn't even have to stretch the truth to get her sympathy said just how terrible their parents had been.

"Of course I don't mind. Your father won't either. You would have had to bring home more than two nice young men to get his attention these days." And someone was still a little bitter over his new hobbies. "Maybe if one was a girl and a stripper."

"Mother!"

"Well, he's been in that workshop of his for a solid week, trying to figure out how to do something with the joints on those stupid birdhouses. Last month was the little stools that are all slightly lopsided. He's driving me crazy. Do you need a stool? I still have four."

"No." She was not going to do that to me. I'd managed to avoid those so far, and I wasn't going to get stuck with any of them.

She sighed. "Goodwill told me I couldn't donate the other ones. I think they're still mad about the bookshelves."

Deciding that changing topics was probably a good idea, I brought the conversation back around to Sunday. "I don't know what you've planned, but the guys want to learn to grill, and I said that I'd see if you were good with us doing steaks or something like that?"

"Of course, that's fine. But they've never grilled?" Considering it was the only way my father could cook food without burning it, I could understand her surprise.

"Nope, they barely boil water." So I was slightly exaggerating on that one—but not by much.

"Those poor dears."

They were going to be mothered to death.

Before she could get back around to the furniture or whatever else he was doing that made her nuts, I decided to retreat. "I've got to get some paperwork done, but I'll call you back later in the week to iron out the time. Love you."

"Love you too, and I can't wait to meet your young men." My parents were insane, but I knew how good I had it, so I wasn't going to complain.

At least, not too much.

Getting off the phone before she could change her mind about letting me escape, I hung up and set it down on the table. It was just after seven—so not late enough for bed. But I felt unsettled and wasn't sure what else I wanted to do, besides the mountain of paperwork that was piling up.

Part of the problem was the silence after having Sawyer and Cooper over most of the weekend. They were anything but quiet. I loved it. Cooper's mild chaos and Sawyer's steady presence—well, until Cooper got him riled up—were perfect. They were so funny.

But it made my time away from them feel much more…alone.

At the rate that Cooper texted, I shouldn't be lonely, but it wasn't the same. The chime of my phone had me smiling. "Speak of the devil."

Standing up, I reached for the phone and headed for the kitchen. Opening the text message, I barked out a laugh. "How did he talk you into that, Sawyer?"

Some kind of bribe—or more than likely, something that he'd need to be punished for.

And knowing Cooper, he'd already thought about that. Something about being restrained and denied made his need and energy just go right into overdrive. Smiling at the picture, I couldn't take my eyes off it. It was cute and sexy as hell. My cock was already achingly hard from just picturing my two boys.

I still wasn't sure how Cooper had talked him into it, but there, standing side-by-side, were my boys, pants down to their thighs while they took a bathroom mirror selfie of their trapped cocks. Texting him as I walked into the kitchen, I grinned as I responded.

My boys look so sexy, but you'd better not be trying to play with yourselves. I know you remember the rules.

Setting the phone on the counter, I started digging around in the fridge. I found some leftover chicken and went about making a stir-fry to go with it. Before long, I heard my phone go off. Too curious to wait, I walked over to see what my handful was up to now.

We're being good Master…and we have our cages on, so we can't play with our dicks…but kissing is allowed…right?

A string of cute and dirty emojis followed, and I could

only attempt to guess what he meant. From the little wiggly butt that was shaking on my screen, though, Cooper didn't mean kissing on the mouth.

Before I could even think of what to say, my phone chimed again, that time from Sawyer. It was short and to the point.

He's making me crazy.

There were no cute little characters from Sawyer, but I could guess right away what Cooper was up to. Texting Sawyer back first, all I could do was shake my head at Cooper's antics.

Is he trying to figure out a way to come or a way to get punished and hoping I'll let him come after?

Switching screens, I went back to Cooper.

If you make Sawyer crazy, I'm going to let him orgasm first.

Cooper responded in seconds.

That's mean...I've been so good...is he going to get to come when you go on your date?? I've been so good...can we have kisses?

More dirty emojis filled the screen after his actual words, and I knew I was going to have to look up the meaning to some of them.

Sawyer's text came in before I could begin deciphering Cooper's hieroglyphics.

Both. Anything. He's horny and bored. And he started picking out classes at his school today, so it's making him antsy.

Ah, that made sense.

How about you have him get into his gear, and his pup can play ball for a while?

Rewarding Cooper when he was deliberately driving Sawyer nuts wasn't a good idea, but a distraction was clearly in order. Switching back, slightly frustrated to have to keep going to different screens, I texted Cooper.

I'm not sure you've been good enough for kisses. Especially the naughty kind you're hinting at.

More like begging for, but that wasn't the point.

There was nothing back from Sawyer yet, which was slightly concerning, but Cooper responded right away.

He's a tattletale.

Laughing, I finally saw the message from Sawyer come in. Going back to his screen and reading his message, I was starting to wish he used more of the funny little pictures, so I could have guessed what he was feeling.

I offered, but he thought it would be weird without you with him.

Not willing to guess how he'd taken that, I texted back.

How did that make you feel? I don't want to come between the time you spend together.

Reminding myself that communication was key and not to feel bad about things changing between them...because change wasn't always bad, I waited to see what he would say. When his text came back after a long silence, I was relieved.

I understood it. It's different now that you play with him, and I get to curl up with you. I don't mind. You make everything better with us. You don't come between us.

It was a long text for Sawyer, and I wished he was with me, so I could pull him into a hug. Texting back, I decided to try one of Cooper's ridiculous emojis. Sending an odd, smiling little creature who seemed to be hugging an imaginary person, I hoped Sawyer got the message.

I like it when you curl up with me. You both have made my life much richer, and I have to admit, when you're not here, I miss you.

Going back to Cooper, I'd finally figured out what to tell him.

How about you talk Sawyer into having pup time? I'm sure he'd like to cuddle with you.

Cooper's response popped up immediately.

That's a great idea!

None of the little icons made sense that time, so I

ignored them. When the quiet from both boys stretched out into several minutes, I went back to finish dinner. It was a bit maddening not knowing what was going on, but I wasn't going to let myself stalk them.

Because I didn't have to.

When they finished talking, Cooper would let me know exactly what had happened. I wasn't sure if the constant chatter was his way of keeping me involved or just part of his personality, but I was rapidly becoming addicted to knowing what was going on in their life away from me.

By the time the stir-fry was done, which wasn't really that long, I heard my phone go off. Taking my phone and my plate to the table, I swiped the screen and warmth filled me as I saw what Cooper had sent.

It was a picture.

Sexy but not just another random dick pic, Cooper had taken a very awkward photo of Sawyer. He was curled up in his puppy gear, head resting on Cooper's lap with his face pointed away from the camera. I got a beautiful shot of Sawyer's back and then down to his legs that were curled up under him with his little tail sticking out. It must have been hard for Cooper to get the shot, but it was worth it.

Sawyer was beautiful.

When I pulled myself away from the picture and actually started to read the message, I was even more touched.

Sawyer said I could send the picture…just not his face…isn't he such a cute pup…so cuddly…he was a little embarrassed about showing you but he didn't tell me no when I got the phone out…isn't he so cute…I can't wait until you see him in person as a pup…haha that was funny…

Sawyer had let him send the picture.

I knew how hard that would have been for him. But just like when he'd dragged the puppy bed over to curl up on, I knew it was his way of showing me he was trying to open up, and that he was getting there.

I kept telling him there was no rush, and I meant it. But I couldn't wait for the moment when he finally showed me, because I knew that was when he would be all in. No more holding back and no more second-guessing what we were doing.

Responding, my eyes kept going to the picture.

Tell my pup that Master said he's beautiful.

Even if he wasn't quite ready yet, they were both my perfect, funny, sweet pups.

10

COOPER

I still hadn't decided if it was a good idea or not. Jackson hadn't said no and hadn't even really been worried, aside from pointing out that she was bossy and nosy, so there was probably nothing wrong. It was just weird.

I was having lunch with Melissa.

Sawyer hadn't been able to think up a rational reason not to go—well, for me not to go. He'd flat-out refused. He'd admitted that she seemed sincere when she'd explained she wanted to get to know us, but then he'd also said that it probably meant giving me the third degree in questions.

I wasn't sure if that was a bad thing, though.

Sure, there would be some stuff that I wouldn't talk about. Topics that Sawyer would lose his marbles over, and things that Jackson probably didn't want his sister to hear about. But she'd researched pups and knew people like us...or at least knew other people in slightly unconventional relationships. So I guess that made me curious too. I wanted to know more about what she knew and what she thought of us.

As I stood outside the sandwich shop that was halfway between her work and mine, I took another deep breath and forced myself to walk in the door. It was going to be fine. I would act like a real adult who was calm, and not slightly over-caffeinated already, and she'd be nice to me. She'd been polite to us when she'd been driving Jackson crazy, so lunch was going to be great.

"Cooper." Melissa's voice rang across the busy restaurant, but it still took a second to find her at the back of the room.

When she'd said we could meet at a small sandwich place I was thinking something…less busy. It was cute and smelled delicious, but it was packed. Looking around, I had to wonder if their whole family had a thing for quirky little restaurants.

Making my way over to Melissa, she smiled and seemed excited to see me. I grinned and looked around. "Hi, this is packed."

She nodded. "It's usually pretty crazy around lunch. I got here a few minutes ago and managed to grab a table. You go order over there. If I get up, we'll lose the table in this madhouse, so you go first and then I will."

"Okay, sure. I'll be right back." The line looked long, but it moved quicker than I expected. Within a few minutes, we both had food and were back at the table.

Eating and small talk gave me space to relax. By the time she started to turn the conversation toward the real things she was curious about it, I was actually ready to talk.

"You have no idea how surprised I was when after all his drama that I found out he'd met you guys through that ad mix-up." Melissa scrunched up her face, looking guilty. "And I'm not sure if I said it to you guys, but I'm really sorry about that."

"Jackson explained everything, and yeah, if you think

you were shocked, picture how we felt. He actually emailed us back and was so sweet and nice it was amazing." Taking a sip of my drink, I thought about what she'd said. "What kind of drama?"

Laughing, she set her sandwich down. "He was so angry at me. He came storming into my house, losing his marbles. Jackson had been convinced that I'd done it on purpose." She shook her head and a serious expression came across her face. "But I hadn't. I'd never mess with people in the lifestyle like that."

I wasn't sure if she was a worrier or just wasn't confident that I believed her, but I nodded. "No, I get it. Jackson explained, and with your books and all, I can see how it happened."

She looked slightly less worried as she shrugged. "It was late. I should've just gone to bed, but I wanted to get the ads done for a new release."

"So you really do write about"—I glanced around and dropped my voice—"puppy play and that kind of stuff? I mean, I've seen books online and stuff but…"

But I'd never thought I'd meet anyone who actually wrote about it.

That seemed slightly rude, though, like I was calling her weird or something. Melissa grinned; she seemed to understand exactly what I was thinking. "I like figuring people out and…I don't know…I like telling stories, but the people in my head just aren't as vanilla as a lot of other authors."

"So you have kinky people in your head?" I was starting to feel like the most normal person at the table. That was just funny.

She snorted and gave me a snarky look that I'd only seen her aim at Jackson. "I'm not nuts."

Nodding very seriously, I gave her an understanding smile. "Of course not."

Melissa barked out a laugh, startling several people around us. "It's no wonder he loves you. You fit right in with the rest of the family."

"You think he loves me?" The fitting in part was interesting too, but not what caught my attention.

"He's never gotten this serious about anyone this fast. He's like, all ready to set up house and keep you. It's really cute."

Aww. "You don't think it's too fast?"

Shaking her head emphatically, Melissa's expression turned serious again. "Not a chance. I know people outside of the lifestyle might not get it, but when you share a personal and special part of yourself with someone, it speeds up the whole getting-to-know-you process." She shrugged. "Once you've seen someone in a diaper or with a tail, you move past the stupid shit really fast."

Before she'd even finished, I started to choke. Coke went down the wrong way, and all I could do was cough and try to figure out how to breathe.

"Are you okay?" She asked it several times before I was finally able to nod.

Answering her with words took a bit longer. "I'm fine, sorry, just swallowed funny."

Once she was sure I wasn't going to pass out, her snark returned. Rolling her eyes, she sighed. "If you choke to death or I have to call an ambulance, he'll never let us go anywhere else together."

I leaned back in my chair and responded dryly. "Sorry to ruin your schemes."

"You should be. I have plans that don't involve you being dead."

Laughing, I shrugged. "To be honest, I'm more curious about Jackson's plans than yours."

She thought Jackson loved us.

Yeah, I was much more curious about Jackson's plans than hers.

"PEOPLE ARE STUPID." PLOPPING DOWN IN ONE OF THE small chairs in the back room, I glanced at April, who'd followed me in. "Why do people want caffeine this late in the evening? Sawyer would kill me if I was drinking coffee at this point in the day."

He wouldn't just be mad, he'd tell Jackson on me—then I'd never get out of the blasted cage.

Shoving the sexy fantasy that tried to form out of my mind, because I knew that would just lead to frustration, I let my head fall back against the wall. April just smiled. "He loves you too much to even blink."

"He says I'm a menace when I've had too much caffeine." Sawyer might have had a few other choice words to say on the subject, and Jackson had just guilted me into doing better about not overdoing it on the coffee. I actually listened—most of the time.

"I just can't believe that." She sat down on a chair across from me. As she leaned forward her hair moved, and I could see the bottom layer that was still brightly colored peeking out from under the top layer, which so dark that it was almost black.

She probably wouldn't believe a lot of things about Sawyer and me, but I wasn't going to push it. "He's funny when he gets worked up."

"Now that I can believe." April smiled and stretched out. "What's he doing tonight?"

Probably getting fucked.

"Hanging out with a friend." It wasn't exactly lying, but the answer still made me uncomfortable.

Keeping the puppy part of my life private wasn't an issue. I didn't need to share it to feel like I was being honest about who I was. Some things weren't anybody else's business. But not mentioning that we were dating Jackson felt wrong...like I was ignoring him or denying that he was a special part of our life.

I had a feeling Sawyer would have a heart attack, though.

He was getting more comfortable about opening up with Jackson and admitting that Jackson was important to him. The fact that he let me take the picture of him curled up as his pup was huge. When Jackson had said that letting Sawyer have time as a pup might be a good idea, I knew it was perfect immediately.

It gave Sawyer a chance to relax and me something else to focus on besides my trapped cock. I hadn't been sure that I actually wanted to ignore the cage, but Sawyer had been getting annoyed with me.

I liked the crazy needy feeling that would run through me when I started thinking about sex and couldn't actually get hard. It was insane. I knew I was turned-on. I could feel everything in me want to get erect, but the cage prevented it, and that was just an immediate reminder that Jackson had put it on me.

Knowing I belonged to Jackson like that was...erotic... special....We were his boys...his pups.

The most incredible sight I thought I would ever see was Sawyer laid out on the bed and watching Jackson with wide, emotion-filled eyes as Jackson slipped the cage over his cock. Sawyer had asked for it—or at least said something to let Jackson know it was what he wanted.

He knew we both belonged to Jackson.

"Cooper, are you even listening to me?" April was grinning when her words caught my attention.

"Yes?" Judging by the way she was looking at me, though, I thought the answer was probably no.

"I asked you what Sawyer and his friend are doing." One eyebrow went up, and she smiled. "Twice."

"Oh. Um, sorry." Shrugging, I tried to look casual. "They're going out to dinner and to hang out since I'm working late."

"That's good. Neither of you seems to do anything with other friends a lot." Her smile dimmed slightly. "I know you guys love each other, but don't forget you need stuff that's just for you."

For other couples, I knew that was true, but I wasn't sure that applied to the two of us...or the three of us.

There wasn't anything specific I could pin down, but I'd never felt like I needed anyone else. Sure, I liked talking with April and the other people I worked with, but aside from the occasional invite to something, they were basically just work friends.

Sawyer didn't even really want that. He'd made it very clear that he needed the people at work to stay there. I think in his mind, the less they knew about us, the safer we were.

He was probably right.

But I think the biggest thing was that when he wasn't around, I missed him.

"We like doing things together. He's my best friend, not just my boyfriend or something casual like that. It's different. Besides, I'm starting school soon, so I have that and it's just for me." Shrugging, I decided changing the subject might be a good idea.

April was getting curious and if I wasn't careful, she

was going to ask something that I wasn't sure how to answer...not without oversharing. "Have you heard anything about the new location yet? Any good gossip about what they're doing?"

She didn't look happy about the change in subject, but she didn't stop me. "Maybe. I was talking with someone the other day and they said that the bigwigs were out looking at some locations recently. Evidently, they've got it narrowed down to a few choices now, but I'm not sure where."

"That's better than I'd been imagining. Any idea what the timetable looks like?" With school starting in just a few weeks and everything all ironed out with that, I was starting to feel a little more confident that I'd come across like a functional adult...at least on a résumé.

She laughed and shook her head. "You already know the answer to that."

Giving her a big grin, I shrugged. "But eventually, I'll ask and you'll be able to say that you know something."

"You're like that kid on a car trip who keeps asking if we're there yet."

Grinning, I shrugged. "Yup, that would be me."

"You must drive Sawyer crazy." She was laughing, probably teasing, but I nodded.

"Some days, yes." There was no point in lying about that.

"Hey, before I forget, I saw that you put in a request to change your schedule on Sunday and work first thing in the morning again. Are you sure? That shift sucks." April had meant it as an innocent question, but she'd inadvertently brought up something else difficult.

We were going to meet Jackson's parents.

"Sawyer and I are going over to a friend's house for a barbecue. Is the switch a problem?" There was the tiniest part of me that perked up at the idea of having to cancel the plans.

It wasn't a huge fear or even something that I was worrying over, but it was still going to be weird. Jackson was sure his parents wouldn't have an issue. I was having a hard time imagining that. My experience with parents hadn't left me quite as confident as he seemed to be.

People came around and after a while realized the mistakes they'd made. But I didn't want Jackson to have to deal with that. Knowing that both Jackson and Melissa were so confident it would be all right made it easier, though.

April nodded. "That's fine. It's good you guys are getting out of the house. Up until recently, when I asked what you had planned, the answer was always nothing. You two were the biggest homebodies I knew."

Because Jackson liked taking us places.

He had lists of things in his head that he thought we would love. Like the amusement park last weekend. Sawyer and I weren't so crazy poor anymore, but we'd had to be careful for so long that we didn't think about going places.

Sure, we'd go to the movies occasionally, or we'd go out to eat, but I really did prefer watching a movie at home with delivery. April was just one of those people who always liked going places and doing things. "I like being home."

"Sometimes you're like a five-year-old in a twentysomething's body, and other times it's like you're fifty." She stood up and stretched. "You have a few more minutes, but I want to check on a couple of things. Take your full break."

"Got it." I wasn't going to argue about getting to stay off my feet longer. "We're still on for going over those reports after my shift, right?"

Working late wasn't what I wanted to be doing, but it would be important if I ever got the manager's position. I wanted to go in knowing as much as I could about the store and not start confused and feeling like I was already behind.

April turned as she was walking out the door. "Yes, you catch on quick, so it might not take us that long."

Getting home early sounded wonderful. I was more than ready to see what my guys were up to and to figure out what I could talk Jackson into. I wasn't sure exactly what I wanted, but it had been days since I'd come, and I couldn't wait to tell him what a good boy I'd been.

11

SAWYER

"You know...if I wanted to drive Cooper nuts, I could tell him that we went for sushi." I gave Jackson a slightly Cooper-ish smile, loving the way he shook his head and grinned.

"Has he been that bad?"

"You have no idea. Well, maybe you do. All those pictures and..." Once everything clicked in my head that I was talking with Jackson about sending him a dick pic I found myself blushing.

Jackson reached over and took my hand. "I loved two particular pictures. I'm sure you can guess which ones."

Embarrassed but not willing to back down, I glanced at my plate but kept talking. "I told him he couldn't show my face."

"Like the rule for the puppy photo?" Once Jackson had seen that I was nervous but not unwilling to talk, he'd kept pushing.

He had made it very clear in the past that safewords weren't just for when we were having sex, and I knew I could stop the conversation at any time. Maybe I was simply less stressed than I'd been about it all originally, or maybe I was just more comfortable with him, but the need to clam up was a lot less intense.

"Yes. I thought you might want to see a bit and…and so when Cooper got the phone out, I didn't tell him no." I thought naked photos were stupid, but since the two pictures hadn't included my face and you really couldn't tell who it was, I'd given in.

Then laughing, I finally glanced back up at Jackson to see him smiling tenderly at me. "But when he wanted to do a whole series and pretend to be a real photographer, I put a stop to it."

Jackson's smile widened, and he started to laugh. "You don't want to be my sexy naked model?"

"Um, no. Just those two were weird." Shrugging, I went back to playing with my potato. "He feels daring and sexy when he does it, and sometimes he just gets stupid excited over something, but it's more awkward for me."

"Just remind Cooper that you don't want to. I loved the two he sent me, but I don't want you to do anything that makes you uncomfortable." Jackson squeezed my hand, and I felt his fingers start caressing it. "It's been easy to see that he likes the cock cage. How has it been for you?"

Fuck.

When Jackson had originally asked for a booth at the back of the restaurant that had some privacy, I'd known he wanted to talk about more interesting topics than just the weather. That didn't make it any easier, though.

The cock cage.

I wasn't sure how to describe it. Taking a deep breath, and possibly holding on to Jackson too tight, I just jumped right in. "I like it."

And that was a toe in the water and not the belly flop I'd imagined.

Forcing myself to go again, I looked down at Jackson's hand wrapped around mine. "I like feeling like I belong to you. I know the one item doesn't change anything really, but it feels like it does."

"It's giving me a lot more control. Even though you weren't able to orgasm before without permission, now you've given me the ability to decide when you get hard." Jackson's voice was deeper, and as I glanced up at him, I could see the desire building inside him.

"You like it."

Well, *duh*, it'd been his idea, but…

Jackson nodded, smiling, but not losing the arousal that was wrapping itself around him. "More than I thought I would. When I'd originally started thinking about the toy and researching it, I wasn't sure how it would feel. But I'm not going to lie—I love knowing that you belong to me on that basic a level. It's…powerful, not like power hungry but more like…special and important."

"For me too." Losing my nerve, my gaze fell back to our hands. "I know for Cooper, the feeling of being owned makes him turned-on and crazy hot. I think for me, it's not really about the desire that it amplifies, but it's more like the feelings I get when I'm a pup…quiet, centered…I don't know if I'm explaining it right."

Trying to describe things like that always made me feel stupid—like I didn't know enough English to get my point across. It was as if there were a whole bunch of words that would be perfect, but they were just out of reach.

He leaned over and gave me a kiss on the cheek. "Don't put yourself down. I can see those negative thoughts flying across your face. You explained it very well. You and Cooper are completely different people, and I wasn't expecting you both to have the same reaction. I'm extremely proud of you for admitting what you wanted and telling me how it feels."

His fingers released me, but before I could even miss it, his hand came down to rest on my leg. The simple touch sent a flood of sensation through me. That was another fun fact about the cage, most of the time it was calming, but once I started to get turned-on, it seemed to magnify everything.

It was all I could do not to groan as his finger started absently caressing my leg. Jackson kept talking like it was nothing, but meeting his gaze, I realized he knew exactly what he was doing.

But I wasn't sure if I was relieved that he was taking things in a naughtier direction or not.

I was hoping it meant I was going to get to come, but after being trapped for several days, I wasn't going to assume. Thinking back to what he'd just said, it was hard to get my brain to function. What had he been saying? Oh, he was proud of me.

"Um, thank you. I...it's..." The words didn't want to come out. It took entirely too much brainpower to sit still while his fingers kept wandering higher, toward my dick. "I like...making you proud."

The hand that was wandering over me stilled while he ate a bite of his steak. It gave me time to make my brain work, but instead of feeling more embarrassed, something inside me loosened. "Having that physical proof of our relationship makes it easier for me. Talking to you about stuff isn't as hard, and even letting Cooper talk me into embarrassing things is easier."

"Like sending me a picture of your sexy, trapped cock." He said it simply, like he was stating a fact, and his hand wasn't even moving, but something about it pushed me back toward the aroused and confused side again.

"Um, yes...it was sexy?" My brain really wasn't working. Not that Jackson seemed to mind.

No, Jackson seemed to be thoroughly enjoying himself. His hand started to move again. The slow exploration in the direction of my dick made me want to moan and beg for more. Jackson's voice dropped lower, and it sent sparks through me. "It was very sexy. It was my boys showing their master their trapped cocks. And I knew how hard it would be for you, so that made it even hotter."

His fingers were finally at the edge of the cage, and I was suddenly grateful he'd tucked me in the back of the booth facing away from most of the restaurant. If it'd been packed, people would still have been able to see me, but on a Wednesday night, the place was only half-full.

"Getting you boys tucked into your cages was incredible, and seeing you both wearing them was even better, but knowing how it made you feel makes it special." He pressed another kiss to my cheek, but the sweet touch of his lips was at odds with the wicked things his fingers were doing.

Caressing just around the base of the restraint, he wasn't touching my cock, but it was close enough that it was sending delicious sparks through me. Jackson's words didn't help either. "And hearing from Cooper how turned-on he was and reading his dirty texts about the kisses he wanted made my cock so hard it hurt."

Jackson was trying to kill me.

I was an idiot. "Kisses?"

Jackson's dirty chuckle made me shiver. "Yes, Cooper wanted to know if kisses were allowed, but he didn't mean on your face." His voice grew quieter, and he leaned closer. "The naughty boy wanted to bend you over and see what would happen if he kissed and licked around your hole. He's been reading dirty things online. But I told him no. I wanted to be with my boys when they got to come next."

Fuck.

I moaned. It was low, and I stopped it as soon as I realized what I was doing, but Jackson heard it. My eyes slammed shut, but I could hear the devilish grin on his face when he spoke. "It sounds like you approve of that idea. Have you been reading dirty things online too?"

My head nodded without me even thinking about it. I couldn't decide if my brain was tattling on me or if it was my trapped cock, but it was impossible to hide it from him. Jackson's hand finally moved to drape over my cage and the way it shifted made me fight to sit still.

"I bet you've been looking at wicked things. Maybe watching porn online where a master has his sexy boy locked away and won't let him come?" Before I could even figure out how to respond, Jackson continued his wicked teasing. "I bet you've been thinking about how Cooper looked running around with his tail wagging and his cage on."

Yes.

Yes.

Yes.

The words wouldn't come out, though. But a needy whimper did.

Jackson's fingers trailed down over the cage to play with my balls, and it felt so incredible, I wasn't sure I could breathe. Almost painful, but not in a bad way—they were sensitive, and it was close to the same feeling as when he'd spanked me.

"Do you want to know how it feels to come, still trapped in your cage? Do you want to know how it feels to have that incredible pleasure when you orgasm but not feel the rush of cum as it shoots out of you?" My sweet, attentive boyfriend might have picked me up for our date, but it was clear that my wicked, dirty master would be the one to take me home.

Thank God.

I loved being caged and knowing how much he loved it made it even better, but I was ready to come. So ready, I actually found the words. "Please."

Well, word.

But Master was happy, and that was all that mattered. "My good boy, I love it when you're open with me and tell me what you want." Master's hand pushed between my legs, forcing me to spread myself open for him.

Fuck.

His finger started caressing the sensitive spot between my balls and ass, and all I could think about was coming. "See what kind of rewards you get when you're a good boy for Master?"

He was going to kill me.

When I got one last caress, and he slowly moved his hand away, I whimpered. Jackson chuckled. "Naughty boy, the waiter is coming, and he doesn't need to see how needy my sexy boy is."

Shit.

My eyes popped open, and I sat up straighter in the seat. How had I forgotten where we were? Pure pleasure rolled off Jackson as he watched me try to look functional in the seconds before the waiter came around the side of the booth.

Crazy need was still bouncing around in me as the man started to speak. "And how are your steaks, gentleman?"

Thankfully, Jackson took the question. "Delicious, thank you."

The tall, quiet waiter nodded. "Please let me know if there is anything else I can get for you."

"Of course, but I think we're fine for now." Jackson's words were smooth and even. There was no hint at all that he'd been whispering dirty things to me or that he'd been feeling me up under the table. The images running through my head and the rush of naughty arousal made it even harder to think.

"I'll check on you later then." Nodding and giving us a bland smile, he walked away.

"I'm not sure it's a good idea for him to check on us later. Who knows what I might be doing to you when he comes back." Jackson's hand went back to my cage-covered dick. "Open your legs again. I wasn't done playing with my boy yet."

The full spectrum of emotions ran through me as I spread wider for him. I felt dirty and beautiful at the same time, and the desire that pounded away at me only seemed to magnify when there was nowhere for it to go.

"Eat your dinner. I can't take you home if you're still hungry." It shouldn't have been sexy, but something about the implied threat in his voice that he'd keep me here, turned-on and needy, for as long as he wanted was stupid hot.

With shaking hands, I managed to take several more bites, but as one finger dipped down and teased over my hole, I had to set the fork down. Even through the layers of clothing, it was incredible. "Please..."

"What do you need?" Jackson's wicked smile said he knew exactly what he was doing to me.

I had a feeling that hints and embarrassment were not going to be good enough to get me home in a timely manner and fucked—and that was what I wanted. "Take me back to the apartment, Master. Please make love to me."

Leaning in and giving me a quick peck on the lips,

Jackson pulled away smiling. "If that's what my good boy wants for his date, then let's go."

The relief that rushed through me as he spoke was staggering.

I loved going out with Jackson, but watching him get the check so we could leave was the best part of the date. In minutes, he had us out the door and back in the car. But if I thought his teasing at the restaurant was bad, privacy made it even worse.

As we pulled out of the parking lot and onto the main road, Jackson's hand came back to my thigh. "Open your pants for me. I want to see what your sexy, trapped cock looks like again." His fingers teased and caressed up my leg as he continued the dirty talk. "I wanted to strip you down as soon as I picked you up, but I knew that if I did, we'd never leave the apartment."

Trying to make my arms work enough to get my hands to my pants, I listened as Jackson's naughty words turned sweet. "But I like taking you out and doing things with you. I like having our time together."

My fingers finally started to open my pants, but the flashes of headlights had my heart pounding in my chest. Jackson finally moaned as I pushed my briefs down just enough to for him to see the cage covering my cock.

When we pulled up at a light seconds later, I covered my cock up again. Jackson shook his head. "There's no one here. Let me see it again. You look so sexy, baby."

Letting out a moan that was part embarrassment and part arousal, I pushed them down again. Jackson's hand moved to cover my cock, and I could feel his fingers start to caress my balls as the car began to go again.

As they inched lower down my body, Jackson didn't seem to mind when I released the fabric and gripped the seat instead. His hand and my dick were covered, but if anyone had glanced at the car, they would have known something was up.

With my head thrown back and the desperate fight not to shove myself against his touch and beg for more, it must have been clear how aroused I was. Cooper was usually the exhibitionist in the bunch, but the idea that someone might see us was insanely erotic.

By the time we were pulling into the parking lot, Jackson had one finger circling my opening, and he was telling me all the crazy things he'd been fantasizing about. Master had a dirty imagination and wasn't afraid to let it show.

He begrudgingly let me straighten my clothes as he stopped the car, but I knew his teasing had only paused long enough to get us to the apartment. The walk across the parking lot and up the stairs had never been longer. I'd grown used to the feeling of being locked away, but now every movement and sway of my cock brought my attention back to the cage.

I'd half expected Jackson to throw me up against the door as soon as it closed behind us, but much to my disappointment, he'd found his patience again, damn it.

Jackson led me over to the couch, and sitting down, pulled me into his lap. As I straddled his legs, his hands wrapped around me to start kneading at my cheeks. Tugging me close, he took my mouth in a slow, deep kiss that had me moaning in his arms.

Easing away to nibble on my lips and kiss along my jaw, Jackson's fingers started caressing the area around my hole, pulling my cheeks apart so I felt empty and aching to be filled. I moaned and whimpered as he continued to kiss and tease me.

When I was shaking and fighting to stop myself from thrusting my ass back harder into his hands to demand more, Jackson finally reached around to unbutton my clothing. A confused sort of relief flooded through me as he shoved my pants and briefs down my legs. The combination of being aroused and naked, but still trapped and unable to get hard was confusing but hot.

My moan echoed through the room when Jackson brought his hands around to start playing with my ass again. My cock was fighting to get hard, pressing against the smooth cage. Everything in me wanted to feel more of his touch and to have his dick slide deep inside me. I knew how good it would feel, and it was all my body could focus on.

"That's my sexy boy. Let me hear how good it feels." Master's rough words sent me even higher as he started rocking my hips so my cage rubbed against his cock.

When the tip of one finger pressed against my hole, the words just came tumbling out. "Please. Master. Please. Touch. Yes. Please."

Jackson chuckled. "What do you want? What does my sexy boy want from his master?"

"Please. Yes. Please." Real words just wouldn't come out. My head fell to his shoulder, and another moan tore out of me as he eased the tip right inside my ass. The clenched muscles stretched, and it was the barest hint of what was to come, but it was enough to fry my brain.

I was so lost in the flood of sensations, it took Cooper's excited voice coming from entirely too close before I realized he was home.

"God, that's hot. I knew you guys would finally learn what to do when I wasn't around."

12

JACKSON

Standing by the couch, Cooper looked excited at the hope of getting to come, but also incredibly proud of us. It was like he was pleased that we'd managed to get turned-on and naughty without him having to prod us.

He was so funny.

Nibbling on Sawyer's neck, I pulled away to smile at Cooper. "Welcome home. We had a good time at dinner."

Cooper wiggled his eyebrows up and down in a bad imitation of a dirty leer. "I can see." Then his leer became a naughty pout. "Do I get to play too, or am I still being punished, Master?"

Shallowly fucking Sawyer with my finger so he would make that beautiful moan again, I watched Cooper. "Have you been a good boy?"

Cooper gave me that innocent look. "Of course, Master."

Sawyer started to laugh midmoan, and Cooper stuck his tongue out at him. Laughing, I shook my head. "If you're very good tonight, I'll let you come. But I'm not sure I believe that you've been a good boy the entire time your cage has been on."

All Cooper seemed to hear was that he would get to come. "Oh, Master, can I get naked too?"

Pulling out of Sawyer's ass, I gave him a pat and a lingering kiss. "I want both of my boys naked."

Sawyer looked frustrated at the loss of my touch, but he stood up on slightly unsteady legs and started to slowly finish stripping out of his clothes. Cooper, on the other hand, was stripped in seconds. Nearly bouncing across the room from a mix of excitement and to get me to watch his cage dance around, Cooper was standing before me naked before I could even laugh.

When they were undressed and clearly excited even though their cocks were locked away, I stood and pulled them into my arms. "You both look beautiful." Letting my hands slide down to grip their asses, I gave them tender kisses.

Moving my hands so that my fingers were teasing along their cracks, I pulled them even tighter against me. "Cooper's been asking for kisses for days—I think it's time I got to see what he wanted. But no fingers. Just kisses. Is that clear?"

Cooper's eyes lit up, but Sawyer groaned in frustration. Giving his ass a smack, I let my fingers brush over his clenched hole. "If you're good, then I'm going to let you come first."

That promise had a shiver racing through my frustrated sub. He was turned-on and desperate, but he also seemed to love the restraint and the feeling of ownership the cage gave him. "If you're naughty, though, I might have to keep teasing you but not let you come, so you learn who you belong to. Who controls your pleasure, Sawyer?"

His gaze took on an unfocused look, and another shiver raced through him. "You, Master."

The low, sexy words sent a shiver through me that time. "Then show me what I want, Sawyer. Show me how incredible my two boys are going to look."

Before I'd even finished the last word, Cooper was tugging Sawyer down to the ground. My wicked boy had evidently been planning for days what he wanted, because in seconds Cooper had him flat on his back with a pillow under Sawyer's hips and one under his head.

Sawyer's mind must have been fried. It took him a long few seconds to figure out why Cooper had straddled his face backward. When Cooper's head fell between Sawyer's legs, and he wiggled his ass in Sawyer's face, he quickly grasped the picture.

They were the hottest thing I'd ever seen.

Every time I thought things between us couldn't get more incredible or arousing, something would top it. I stood there watching for several minutes while they each tried to turn the other on even more. Finally sitting down beside them on the floor, I started caressing them and telling them how sexy they were.

Running my hands over Cooper's ass and along his back, I circled down to tweak one of his nipples before caressing up Sawyer's body. Most of Sawyer's groin was covered by Cooper's chest, but I could easily play with his nipples and run my hand over Cooper's cock cage, nudging it to make him moan.

Teasing Sawyer at dinner and playing with him on the couch had already made me ready, but watching them making love to each other had me so hard I was going to have the outline of my zipper pressed into my cock.

"Get him nice and ready for me Cooper, I can't wait to slide my dick into his tight body. I want him wet and needy for my cock." They both moaned and started kissing and licking even faster.

I couldn't see exactly what Cooper was doing that was making Sawyer gasp and writhe, but I could see Sawyer's tongue tracing around Cooper's sensitive hole. Occasionally, he'd stiffen his tongue and fuck Cooper with slow thrusts; his goal seemed to be to get Cooper turned-on, but not anywhere near enough to actually come.

I could have watched them for hours, but eventually, Sawyer's need started to get frantic. I could see desire in every movement and in every sound, and all I wanted to do was reward him for being so good. Finally, I gave Cooper's ass a smack. "Is Sawyer ready for me, Cooper? Is his hole nice and relaxed for me?"

Cooper's body was shaking as he climbed off Sawyer and kneeled beside him. His lips were puffy and looked like he'd been well-kissed, and his eyes were filled with desire. I sat up and stretched over Sawyer's sexy, desperate body and gave Cooper a heated kiss.

Pulling away, I brought my hand up and caressed his cheek. "Bring me the lube and condoms, Cooper. I think Sawyer's waited long enough."

Cooper made an excited, needy noise and crawled over to the end table. It was so close to how he looked as a pup, I almost smiled. But the feeling of Sawyer's hand as it touched my leg and started caressing up my body pulled my attention away.

Sawyer's words were filled with desire. "You're still dressed."

Answering him honestly, I smiled. "I like being dressed when you're naked." Reaching up to unbutton my shirt, I watched as his eyes devoured every inch of skin that was revealed. "I like knowing you're displayed for me and ready for my touch. You like being on display for me, don't you, Sawyer?"

He was too turned-on to hide what he wanted. Sawyer nodded and spread his legs for me, silently begging to be taken. My sexy, needy boy.

Cooper hurried back with the items he was sent for and waited patiently while I finished taking off my shirt. When that was off and I rose to get out of the rest of my clothing, they both licked their lips, and Cooper reached out to run a hand over Sawyer's chest.

"Give Sawyer a kiss, Cooper. Right on his lips so he knows how much you love him and how sexy he is." As I finished getting undressed, Cooper turned and leaned over Sawyer, taking his mouth until they were both moaning and breathless.

While they were distracted, I put on the condom and opened the lube. That was the sound that finally pulled them apart. Cooper looked eager and restless, and Sawyer looked needy and frantic. When I moved between his legs, Cooper reached down and pulled them up to open Sawyer for me.

Starting with one lubed finger, I slowly teased around Sawyer's hole and gently pressed against it as I did my best to ignore my own aching body. His body swallowed me in one smooth motion, not fighting me but pulling me in. As he moaned and fought to stay still, I kept stretching him, adding a second finger and then a third until he was shaking and bucking up into my fingers.

When I finally pulled my fingers out and leaned over him, lining my cock up with his needy body, all he could do was make sexy little noises and plead for more. Sawyer was so incredible, even Cooper was shaking. Entering him in one long thrust, I bottomed out as Sawyer cried out in pleasure.

He bowed off the floor and his body clenched around me as I started fucking him in a random rhythm that he couldn't anticipate. Slow…fast…shallow…deep, every thrust pushed him closer to the edge but kept him too confused to come.

He was perfect.

Passion echoed off the walls and his needy pleas were what I'd been imagining all night. Part of me wanted to make it go on for hours, but Cooper's patience would only go so long, and Sawyer would probably slip into subspace if I edged him any further. He was already starting to get that glassy faraway look that said he was almost there. Someday soon I would stretch him out and send him flying, but today I wanted to see him explode.

Pushing my arms under his legs, I lifted him just enough that I hit his prostate with every thrust. Even though he couldn't get hard, his body started to clench around me and I could feel his orgasm racing toward him. Sawyer's pleas turned desperate as he begged to come, but the confusion of not getting hard and the pressure on his cock in the cage held him back.

Catching Cooper's eye, I glanced down at Sawyer's chest. Thankfully, Cooper didn't make me find the words; he just threw himself down on the floor and started teasing Sawyer's nipples with his lips and teeth.

"Now." One more thrust against his prostate and one rough scrape of Cooper's teeth over his nipples and Sawyer shattered.

His body shook, and he cried out, writhing beneath me as the sensations flooded him. Fighting the need that threatened to push me over the edge, I focused on Sawyer and Cooper, determined to give both my boys everything they needed. When Sawyer collapsed back onto the floor, spent and tired. I slowly eased out of him.

Not trusting my body quite yet. I ignored the condom and reached for Sawyer's cage instead. Carefully removing it from around his sensitive cock, Sawyer groaned in relief as it was finally off. Setting the restraint aside, I leaned over and gave Sawyer a tender kiss.

As I pulled away, he reached up and ran a hand over my shoulder and down my arm. "You'll stay the night? After you make love to Cooper? You won't—"

Interrupting him with another kiss, I nodded. "For as long as you want me."

Cooper had been so good but as I sat up and looked at him, he threw himself into my arms. Laughing, I held him tight and tried to keep him from landing on Sawyer. "I think someone is still needy. Are you ready for me?" I let one hand slide down and played with his ass. "Is this what you want?"

Cooper was his honest, perfect self. "Yes, right now… please God, fuck me, yes…"

Every time I thought I couldn't love him any more, he did something that just pushed it higher. I might not have said the words yet, but I knew the feeling and when I looked at my boys, it rushed through me. Bringing my hand down on his ass, the smack and his moan filled the room. "Naughty boy."

That only made his frantic need worse.

"Oh please, another, please, I was so good." He arched his ass, begging for more. All I could do was chuckle and rub circles over the area where I knew my handprint would be.

"Not yet, but if you're very good, I might spank you again. Is that what you want, to feel my cock inside you and my hand making your ass red and pushing you even closer to your orgasm?" Cooper nodded but his teeth came down on his lip to try to contain the begging that I knew wanted to escape.

Running my thumb over his mouth, I shook my head. "I have something better to keep that sexy mouth occupied."

Moving him between Sawyer's legs, I eased his head down toward Sawyer's cock. Cooper knew right away what I wanted and as I scooted back, he stretched out and offered up his ass. Sawyer began writhing, and gasps of desire came out as Cooper teased his sensitive cock. Sawyer couldn't decide if he was too tender or if he wanted to come again, but I knew his balls were still achingly full, and the pleasured pain would be perfect.

Quickly changing out the condom, I started stretching Cooper as he moaned around Sawyer's cock. In minutes, I had my cock lined up to his body. As I pushed into him with one long, slow thrust, I brought my hand down on Cooper's ass.

His head came up, and he cried out, pushing back against me for more. Bringing my hand down again as I bottomed out in him, I gave his head a rough push. "I want that mouth busy, so it can't get you into trouble."

That just made my needy boy even hotter. The demanding words, the rough touch…after being trapped for days, it was almost too much for him. As I pulled almost all the way out and thrust back in again, I could feel Cooper's body start to shake.

"You won't get to come until Sawyer does, naughty boy." I spanked his ass again to send him even higher. He moaned, and I saw his head bob up and down in an acknowledgment of the order. Smacking his ass and fucking him harder, it was all I could do not to come as I kept his desire building.

"Naughty subs who come without permission and who demand to be fucked don't get to come first." The words came out deep and rough, but the way he clenched around me and the sexy noises that escaped said he loved every minute of it.

His little moans and cries must have pushed Sawyer over the edge. One minute he was alternating between fucking Cooper's mouth and writhing as if the sensation was almost too much. The next he was bucking up, and from the sounds both made, he was shooting his cum as Cooper lapped every drop up.

When Sawyer went still and Cooper's head came up, I pulled Cooper's back to my chest and pinned him to me. Cooper cried out as I fucked him even harder and finally started pegging his prostate with every thrust. His cage jerked as I slammed into him, but I left it alone. He wanted more; he wanted that last layer of ownership and claim on him.

When he was finally so close he was shaking and even his cries had turned to breathless moans, I roughly pinched his nipples and nailed my cock against his prostate one last time. "Come."

Cooper's orgasm went through him like fireworks. He trembled, and his cries were so loud I knew every person on their floor heard his pleasure. Finally giving into mine, I stopped fighting the desire that had been beating at me. A few rough thrusts kept Cooper's orgasm firing through him, and I gave in. My orgasm crashed over me, and I wrapped my arms tight as we rode out the sensations that were exploding through us.

When we were both done, Cooper collapsed to one side of Sawyer and I curled up on the other. Draping my hand over Sawyer's chest, I took Cooper's hand in mine and moved it so our hands were resting on Sawyer.

Wrapping myself around my boys, I kissed Sawyer's head and brought Cooper's hand up to kiss his knuckles.

Sawyer yawned and rolled his head, so it pushed against me. That one little gesture seemed to be as much as he was willing to move.

Sawyer's eyes were still closed when he spoke, but he sounded tired and utterly spent. "You're staying the night, right?"

Cooper smiled in agreement, but then looked at me, slightly confused. "My cock cage is still on."

I smiled and nodded. "Because I like it on there. I might put Sawyer's back on before I leave tomorrow. I like knowing my boys will remember who they belong to."

Sawyer blushed faintly and refused to comment, but Cooper beamed and actually sat up to kiss me. "I belong to you, Master."

Lifting my head, I took his mouth in a slow, deep kiss. As I pulled back, I gave him a long look that I hoped said everything I knew Sawyer wasn't ready to hear. I worried for just a moment, but the smile that shone from Cooper's face said he knew what I couldn't say.

Not yet, at least.

13

COOPER

"It's going to be fine. They're going to love you both." The way Jackson was glancing around the car, I wasn't sure if he was talking to me or Sawyer, but I smiled, trying to show him I was fine.

Sawyer nodded, but his death grip on the brownies said he wasn't as calm as he was trying to pretend to be. I understood why they were nervous, but after thinking about it, I'd decided there really wasn't anything to worry over.

People obsessed over the worst thing that could happen. Well, I'd already lived through that—and so had Sawyer, if he'd bothered to think it over. Jackson had already promised that no matter what, nothing would change how he felt about us, and that was good enough for me. If his parents didn't like me, that was just one more bunch on the list. It wasn't worth panicking over.

Besides, Melissa said they were going to love us.

She might love to drive Jackson absolutely nuts, but she didn't seem to have the same drive to torment me, so I had no reason to think she was lying. It was going to be fine. I just had to convince the other two of that.

Or distract them.

"Will you put up the obstacle course again when we get home? I want to see if it feels even better when I'm running through without my cage. But having that on last time was hot. You're going to have to try it sometime, Sawyer."

And *bam*! They were both distracted by something else.

Sawyer immediately switched over to his crazy internal debate about when to show Jackson his pup. Which was just getting silly, really. They were both ready for it, but neither was willing to push it. Jackson, on the other hand, was clearly picturing both of us as pups, running through the course because he reached down and adjusted his cock before putting his hand back on the wheel.

Finally, Jackson realized he hadn't given me an answer. Nodding, he put a hand back over his seat and reached for mine. Giving it a squeeze before he let go, he nodded. "I think that should be fine. The stuff is still in the guest room where we put it, so it will be easy to set up."

Looking at Sawyer who was sitting in the passenger seat, I smiled sweetly. "You're okay with me playing tonight, right?"

Sawyer shot daggers at me.

So I blew him a kiss.

"Cooper, what did you do?" Jackson had that sound in his voice like he was trying to decide if I needed to be punished or not.

It was hot.

There wasn't going to be time for fun punishments, though, so I shook my head and aimed my innocent look right at him. "Nothing."

Not yet, at least.

Jackson clearly didn't believe me, but they were both still so distracted that we'd pulled up in front of a large two-story building before they could start to worry again. As he parked the car, Jackson stopped us before we got out. "They're going to love you both. My mother is excited to meet you, and as long as you say you love his birdhouses or take one of the blasted stools then my father will love you too."

I just grinned. I couldn't wait to see the projects his dad was working on. "We're funny and lovable. It's going to be fine."

Jackson nodded. "Yes, exactly."

They were going to give me ulcers. "Don't they say if you're nervous to picture everyone naked? Well, Jackson, how about you just picture me naked since you're related to everyone else there? And Sawyer, you should already be picturing me naked because I'm fabulous."

Jackson laughed, and Sawyer flopped back against the door, rolling his eyes. "Cooper, you can't say shit like that in front of his parents."

Duh.

"We're not in front of his parents yet. Just Melissa." Waving to her as she walked up to the car, I turned back to Sawyer. "And she probably couldn't hear me."

"She's definitely the one person who wouldn't blink at anything that came out of your mouth, Cooper." Jackson's laughter had faded, but his smile was still wide and relaxed.

Perfect.

"Hey, I behaved at lunch. No crazy stories or anything. I was a real, functional adult." I'd been very pleased about that.

Sawyer snorted. "She was probably disappointed."

Possibly.

But at least we weren't going to end up in a book if we were boring. Not that I really had an issue with that. We were funny and had a great backstory and all three of us were hot...especially Jackson. He really didn't want to end up in one of her books, though, so until I could make sure she'd behave, I had to be careful.

Jackson reached over the seat and took my hand. "You can be yourself around them. I promise."

I lifted one eyebrow and gave him a "Don't be stupid" look. "Do you want to end up in a dirty romance novel?"

Jackson laughed and rolled his eyes. "Okay, I take that back. How about I say not to be so cute we end up in a romance novel, but otherwise, be yourself?"

And that had been my plan all along.

Leaning forward, I gave him a kiss. "You worry too much."

Melissa was standing there with one hip popped out, pretending to look at an invisible watch by the time we got out of the car. "How long does it take you guys to go anywhere if it takes five minutes just to get out of the car?"

Jackson ignored the question. "Did they send you out here to check on us?"

Melissa shook her head but shot the house a disgruntled look. "He's trying to convince me that I need another bird feeder. I've already got three."

Jackson's hands immediately went up in front of him, palms out. "Not it."

Rolling my eyes, because I really couldn't handle the crazy, I butted in. "This is not a game of hot potato."

Jackson gave me a pitiful look. "But I already have three."

"Where?"

"Over by the tree line." His expression turned slightly guilty.

"You have several acres of land—you can handle a

few more birdfeeders." And I was pretty sure I could handle a bored old man who had more time than decorating sense.

Jackson sighed. "But—"

Taking a step closer to Jackson, I gave him a pout. "I'm hungry, and you promised to show me how to use the grill."

Jackson grinned, and Melissa belted out a laugh. He leaned in and gave me a kiss. "My little manipulator."

I just gave him my best wide-eyed stare. "I don't know what you're talking about."

Melissa was just about rolling on the floor. "Don't do that. You look like you're a kid, and my mother will think he just robbed the cradle or something."

Now it was my turn to sigh. "I can behave."

"I know. She's just teasing."

Sawyer snorted. "No, she's not. He does look like a kid when he does that."

But it got me out of trouble, and Jackson kind of thought it was hot, so I wasn't planning on stopping it anytime soon. "Food, Sawyer. I was promised food. And fire."

"If you burn your hair again, all bets are off." Sawyer was looking at me like he was trying to decide the best way to wrap me up and keep me secure.

"Jackson will keep me safe. It's going to be fine." Yup, ulcers.

They were both insane.

"You guys are all nuts. But if you don't want Mom to come looking for you, then you'd better get inside." Melissa started walking toward the house. "There is no way she'll be patient much longer."

Giving Sawyer and me one last kiss each, Jackson put his hands on our backs and guided us up to the steps. It had the same feel as Jackson's did. The porch wasn't the same, and the house was two stories and not one, but I could see where he got his taste from.

As we followed Melissa in, Jackson called out as he was shutting the door. "Mom, we're here."

Jackson's parents' house was probably a little fancier than his, and it was easy to see it was older, probably the house he grew up in, but I liked it. A tall, thin woman came around the corner, from what I thought was the kitchen. "Jackson, what have I said about yelling for me?"

Jackson grinned; it was like he was a kid who was thoroughly enjoying driving her nuts. "Mom, I would like you to meet Sawyer and Cooper. Guys, this is my mother, Charlotte Kent."

"It's nice to meet you both. Please, call me Charlotte." Her smile was warm and genuine, but I could see questions behind her eyes as she watched us.

"Thank you. You have a lovely home." *See? Functional adult.*

Sawyer seemed to be going for the same boring, grownup style compliment. "Thank you for having us over. Something smells delicious."

Ha. We were both fabulous. They were going to love us —once the awkward part was out of the way.

Leading us through the house, Charlotte pointed out things and did her best to be a charming hostess. She was like one of those TV moms. It was a little bit weird. Jackson must have seen something on my face because as her back was turned, he leaned in and whispered. "Company manners when she's nervous. If she gets out more than one fork for dinner, we'll spike her drink."

Trying not to laugh, because that would ruin the image I was going for, I rolled my eyes at him and tried to look like a grown-up. He was not helping. When she was watching, he was all polite smiles and "Yes, work was going great," but when she wasn't looking, he'd wink at Sawyer or would pantomime reading a book while grinning evilly at Melissa.

"Jackson, I don't know what you're doing, but stop egging them on." Charlotte gave him a stern look as she led us out to the back porch.

His innocent look was not nearly as good as mine. "I didn't do anything."

"Your sister is nearly purple, and your young men look like they want to smack you." The quiet, reasonable tone had me running through her words twice.

Oops, caught.

Sawyer and I both smoothed out our expressions, and Melissa sighed. "It's nothing."

I caught myself before I could laugh. She just didn't want to have to tell her mother what Jackson was teasing her about. I was starting to think that I'd missed something interesting by being an only child.

"I'm going to keep an eye on you, Jackson. I'm trying to make a good impression, and you're not helping." She was trying to guilt him into behaving, but that didn't seem to be working. Jackson's eyes still sparkled, and his grin was ear-to-ear.

"I was just smiling at her. I have no idea what you're talking about." We were going to have to practice his innocent act. It could use some work.

Shaking her head, his mother shooed us out the door. "Go introduce Cooper and Sawyer to your father and turn on the grill. I'll be right there."

The backyard was expansive and nicely manicured. A fence around the sides and some large trees at the back gave it a lot of privacy. As we headed over to what looked like a garage, I could hear hammering coming from the building —and an occasional curse word.

Jackson led us through a gate in the fence, with

Melissa still following. I had a feeling she wanted to see everything firsthand, but I wasn't sure if it was because she thought it was interesting or that it would be good in a book.

His dad's back was to us, and all I could see was a tall, broad guy with salt-and-pepper hair. Jackson clearly got his height from both parents but his size from his dad. When the gentleman set down the hammer and started reaching for something else, Jackson called out. "Hey, Dad, we're here."

Jackson's dad turned around, a big smile clear on his face even though he was tucked back in the shadows. "I have something for you."

Jackson groaned.

Melissa started to laugh, and I tried not to react when what I wanted to do was elbow him in the side. Jackson recovered quickly and completely ignored the not-so-subtle bird feeder reference. "I want to introduce you to my boyfriends."

The man nodded several times like he really wasn't sure how to respond. That was better than saying something rude, though, so I didn't really mind. Watching as the man wiped off his hands on a nearby rag and started coming to meet us, I was dumbfounded when he finally stepped into the light.

Then I forgot to be an adult for just a few seconds.

"Holy shit, Jackson, you're going to be hot when you get old."

Oops.

Melissa started to laugh so hard she didn't seem like she could breathe. Sawyer groaned, and his head fell back like he was asking God why he was surrounded by morons. Jackson started to choke, but he really didn't seem that upset, which I was grateful for.

"Sorry, that didn't come out right." I wasn't sure how to fix it.

Jackson's dad blinked at me and then shrugged. "Charlie said I was just supposed to say thank you when the little waiter down at the vegan place said I was a sexy beast and called me 'Daddy.' So I think the same thing still applies. Thank you."

They were all really weird.

"You just look so much alike. I wasn't expecting it. Sorry." Someone really should have warned me.

Yup, this was not my fault. Jackson's father was tall and broad, and Jackson seemed to be an exact copy of his dad. Strong features and a young-looking face were framed by silverish hair around temples that gave him a mature, sexy look.

Who doesn't warn their boyfriend that their father looks like someone who could be in a porn shoot for older daddies? All he needed was a little twink staring up at him.

Yup, this was so not my fault. Jackson and I were going to have a talk when we got home.

Jackson finally managed not to choke to death. "Thank you, Cooper. Dad, this is Cooper and Sawyer. Guys, this is my dad, Daniel."

After some slightly weird handshakes, Daniel led us back into the garage. Before he could show us any of the birdhouses that were stacked around the room, some done and some strangely shaped enough that I wasn't sure, Charlotte came around the corner.

"Daniel, they need to get the grill going, or we're never going to eat. Show the boys your projects later." Her voice was still that same smooth tone, but I could almost hear her rolling her eyes.

Daniel looked over at her and smiled, a huge grin on his face. "Charlie! The little excitable one thinks I'm hot."

Charlotte finally gave in and rolled her eyes. "And you had to tell him that. Every time we go eat at that vegan restaurant he struts around for a week. I'm still not calling you Daddy, Daniel Kent." Then she looked at Sawyer and me, mostly me, and shook her finger at us. "Now, no more inflating his ego—it's big enough."

Sawyer and I were both speechless as she turned and walked back toward the house. "Jackson, come turn on the grill. It's like having teenagers all over again every time you come home, I swear."

"I don't strut." Daniel shook his head like she was crazy.

Jackson brought a hand up to my back. "Come on, I'll show you how to get the grill ready."

"They don't know how to turn on the grill?" Out of all the things that had happened, that one little thing seemed to shock Daniel the most.

Jackson shrugged. "No."

Daniel looked like he just couldn't believe it, so I felt like I had to explain. "Um, my dad wasn't very handy, and my mother didn't like fire so…"

He clearly thought I was from another planet. "He wasn't handy either? What kind of tools can you use?"

I just looked at Sawyer and shrugged. "Um, I've used a screwdriver to tighten the table legs when they got wobbly."

Sawyer snorted. "You did that with a butter knife. I don't think we even own a screwdriver."

"Tattletale." I wanted to look slightly functional after the "You're so hot" debacle.

Sawyer finally seemed to find his voice. "Cooper's dad probably never swung a hammer, and all mine did was use one to punch a few holes in the wall when he was drunk one time. So, we're not terribly handy."

Daniel looked like someone had killed his favorite power tool. "That's just terrible."

I wanted to make him happy, which was probably stupid, so I rushed to speak. "Jackson said he'll teach us anything we want. He's going to show me how to grill."

Sawyer tried to restrain himself, but it was nearly impossible. I could hear him mumble fire under his breath as Daniel started to speak. "Well, Jackson's good at the grill, but no, I'll show you how the tools work. We'll get you boys up to speed in no time."

"Oh, thanks." I thought it sounded like fun, and it probably meant he didn't think I was too nuts to have around, so I was going to go with it. "Does that mean I get to make my own birdhouse?"

Daniel nodded enthusiastically. "Of course, we'll start next time you come over. Charlie said if I kept dragging everyone to the garage today she was going to hide my tools again. It took a week to figure out what she did with my table saw. She looks sweet, but she'll get revenge when you least expect it."

Melissa snorted. "She warned you."

Daniel waved his hand around. "That's not the point. Come on, I need my tools this week, so we're not going to piss her off."

Snickering, Sawyer and I followed the group back to the yard. Jackson and his dad were starting to debate something about the flames, and Melissa decided that they were both wrong and took up a completely different viewpoint. I was betting it was just to make them crazy, because her eyes sparkled. She was having a great time.

Sawyer stepped closer and dropped his voice low while we watched them argue. "I can't believe you called his dad hot."

"It's Jackson's fault." Nodding firmly, I continued.

"You're supposed to warn people when your dad looks like a porn star."

Sawyer snickered. "He looks like all he needs is a motorcycle and a twink wrapped around his waist."

"And a T-shirt that says Leather Daddy, or something like that. What did Jackson say he did before he retired?" I couldn't remember.

Sawyer grinned. "He was some kind of stockbroker."

"That just sounds weird." Looking at the three of them, I had to smile. "We don't seem like the oddest people here. I like that."

Sawyer smiled and took my hand to give it a squeeze. "Me too."

"He's going to teach us how to use power tools." I was kind of excited about that.

"Jackson will kill you if you lose a finger on a saw or do something stupid."

I just waved off his worry. "There'll be lots of supervision. Daniel thinks I'm 'the excitable one.' There's no way he'll leave me alone with the tools."

"We're going to end up with a thousand birdhouses all over the yard, aren't we?" Sawyer seemed to think that was a bad thing.

"Yes, it's going to be great." Smiling as I watched the fire discussion continue to rage, I couldn't help but be glad I was right. I wasn't going to shove my "I told you so" in their faces, but I had a feeling everything was going to be fine.

14

SAWYER

I couldn't decide if I was exhausted or wired. As I curled up on the couch with my head on the armrest, I wasn't sure how I felt. The day had gone great, but it was still overwhelming. I'd slept in since Cooper had to go to work early, and once he'd left, Jackson had come back to bed and cuddled with me for a few more hours.

It had been a lazy, perfect morning, and the afternoon had gone well too. Jackson's parents had been nice, and even though it was clear they were trying to figure everything out, they didn't seem to have an issue with us. They'd even thought Cooper was funny.

The couch shifted as Cooper sat down beside me and then flopped on top of me. "That was great. My fire skills are awesome."

I snorted. "Not burning the house or yourself down is not grounds for crowning yourself king of the grill."

"Sure it is. My steaks were fabulous." Cooper's excitement and happiness were contagious, and I found myself smiling.

"Dinner was great, and the brownies turned out wonderful." Even if I did say so myself.

"The brownies were beyond wonderful. I'm just disappointed there aren't any more left." Cooper's sad voice would have been heart-wrenching if it was true.

"You're just trying to see if we had any extras." I knew better than to fall for his drama, most of the time.

"Do we?"

Jackson came wandering in. "Do we what?"

"He wants more brownies."

Jackson groaned. "No more food for you. You're going to pop."

I could hear the pout in Cooper's voice. "But everything was so—"

Jackson didn't even let him finish. "I thought you wanted the obstacle course set up?"

"Oh, how did I forget?" Cooper bounced off the couch. "I think I left the puppy bag in the car. You get out the stuff, I'll be right back."

As he softly laughed, Jackson's footsteps grew closer. When I peeked open one eye he was crouched down beside me. Leaning in, he gave me a tender kiss. "Long day?"

I shrugged a little, not sure how to answer. "I don't know. Maybe?"

My answer didn't seem to bother him; he just brought his hand up and cupped my cheek. "Overwhelmed?"

Closing my eyes again while his fingers softly caressed my face, his question was easy to answer. "Yes."

"How about you lie down with me while we watch Cooper run around and play?" Jackson's fingers wandered up to my hair, and it felt so good I wanted to moan. "I don't think it will be long before he'll be done. Between work this morning and the barbecue this afternoon, I think he's running on fumes."

"Okay." I wiggled my head a little when he stopped rubbing, and he laughed.

"I will give you all the cuddles you want as soon as I get everything set up." Jackson was starting to stand as I opened my eyes again.

"Do you want me to help?" I wasn't too tired to function. Lying down and relaxing so I could shove everything else to the back of my mind sounded just perfect.

"Nope, I got this." He gave me a quick kiss and headed back toward the guest room.

The puppy beds were still in their corner, but Jackson had said leaving the tunnel and things out would drive him nuts, so they'd been put away. I liked the fact that he didn't feel the need to hide everything about it. Sure, I didn't want to have them out when his parents came over, because that would just be weird. But when it was just us, it was nice to know that he was comfortable with it.

More than comfortable probably, if the smile he was wearing as he came back carrying the tunnel was any indication. I loved the way he looked at Cooper's pup when he was running around, barking and just having fun. Jackson watched him like he was the sweetest, most perfect thing he'd ever seen.

I wanted him to look at my pup that way.

I wasn't jealous exactly; it was just that I knew what I was missing, and I only had myself to blame. I'd kept telling myself that I knew when I'd be ready, but I wasn't so sure anymore. Waiting until I was comfortable sounded like the right answer. Waiting until I knew we were going to be part of his life sounded good too.

But we were past all that—meeting his parents proved that better than anything else.

My mind went back to the barbecue. I'd been outside

helping to clean up toward the end of the evening, and when I'd walked into the kitchen, I heard Jackson and Charlotte talking about us. She'd said she could see why he was so serious about us.

Jackson didn't downplay how he felt or argue with her that it was casual. He'd just grinned and nodded, telling her that we were wonderful, and he could see it really working out with us. She didn't ask about any of the specifics of our relationship or comment about how much younger we were; she just smiled and said she was happy that he'd found us.

Like it was that simple.

Like there was nothing to worry about.

Like, of course, it would work out.

Like we would be a family together.

As he wandered in with more of the rails that Cooper jumped over last time, I couldn't help but imagine how it would be a year from now, two years. Could I really see being in that same spot watching Jackson setting up fun things for Cooper to play with? Could I really see us all together like that?

Yes.

It was a simple answer but a scary one because it opened up a flood of other questions. But none I was going to answer tonight. One crazy-ass decision at a time.

Cooper came bouncing back through the house as Jackson was setting up the course. He grinned and dashed back to the bedroom. "I'll be right back."

Jackson laughed. "I'll be right there."

Climbing off the couch, I stretched. "I'll go help him. You finish setting up, so we don't have an enthusiastic pup waiting to play."

"Thank you. I'll have everything ready when you come back out." Jackson's expression was loving and warm, and there was nothing in it that said he had any other expectations other than to enjoy the evening while I cuddled, and Cooper ran like a maniac.

"Sounds good." As I headed back to the bedroom, I couldn't help but think about the two different pictures in my head. One version of how everything would probably go and another of how I wanted it to go...but it was hard.

It was like those pictures where one thing was changed, and people had to pick out the difference. Only, in this case, the difference was clear.

Pup.

Person.

I still wasn't sure what I was going to do even after I made it to the bedroom. Cooper, on the other hand, had no issues with what he wanted. He was already naked and digging around in the night table for lube.

"Ha, found it." He grinned at me. "We need to put this on the grocery list."

"Sure." That was another thing that I wasn't going to even think about tonight. The fact that we were almost living here.

A naked Cooper bounced over and gave me a kiss. "You're going to help me?"

Smiling because his happiness was infectious, I nodded. "Yes, Jackson is getting everything ready."

"Perfect." Cooper gave me a side glance as he walked over to the bag on the bed and started getting out his things. "I'm not going to tell you what would make tonight even better."

I might have rolled my eyes. "I appreciate that."

"I'm also not going to point out that we met his family and they loved us and he basically told them he planned on keeping us." Cooper shrugged as he got the last of his stuff out of the bag and brought the pile over to the floor. "Nope, not going to mention any of it."

Snorting, and not trying to hide my amusement, I nodded. "Because you're so subtle and you want me to make decisions and come to those realizations on my own."

"Aren't I fabulous?" He blew me a kiss and plopped down on the floor. "Hurry and help me."

I was quiet as I helped Cooper get ready, probably too quiet, but he didn't seem to mind. He started sliding into his puppy persona, and he was so excited he was nearly dancing around the room. Even stretching him and sliding the tail in didn't distract him from his enthusiasm.

When he was finally ready, I gave his ass a pat. "Go find Master."

Cooper barked and tried to lick my face, but I just laughed and stood up. "Go on before he thinks you don't want to play."

Another bark and a wag of his tail had him charging out of the room. I could hear the clomp of his kneepads down the hall and his excited bark as he found Jackson. The little whimper that followed could only mean that Cooper was getting rubs of some kind.

As I picked up the lube and walked over to the bed, I still hadn't decided what to do. I knew what I wanted, but the step seemed huge. I knew Jackson wasn't going to rush me, but for just a moment, I wished he would.

I'd told Cooper not to worry about packing my puppy stuff as we'd packed a bag to stay at Jackson's for the weekend, but as I picked it up to move it, it was still way too heavy. Jackson was a little nuts about wanting us to put our clothes in the drawers he'd cleared out, so it should have been almost empty.

Looking inside it, I wasn't sure if I should be cursing Cooper or kissing him.

There was all my gear, just waiting for me, when I'd told him to leave it back at the apartment. The little brat knew me too well.

Not sure I was ready, but confident I was making the right choice, I started stripping off my clothes. When they were in a neat pile on the bed, I stood there staring at everything, second and third guesses running through my head.

But it really boiled down to something simple. Yes, I was scared, but I wanted to show Jackson that he was part of the family. Hiding a big part of who I was away from him wasn't going to show him that.

Picking up the pieces of gear one by one, I slowly made my way out the door and down the hall. I could hear the noises that were coming from Cooper as he played and from Jackson's laughter and encouragement. Even from the first moment he'd seen Cooper as a pup, there had never been any judgment or hesitation, just wonder and acceptance.

Coming to the end of the hall, I peeked around the corner and saw Cooper dashing through the tunnel. Jackson was sitting on the floor, my bed beside him like he was waiting for me to lie down and relax with him.

Well, that's what I wanted to do...just not exactly how Jackson had planned.

Stepping through the doorway, I watched Jackson glance over at me and his eyes widened. Before he could ask me something that I probably wouldn't be able to answer, I spoke quietly. "Will you help me get ready?"

I could see emotions and all kinds of questions running through his mind, but he smiled and nodded as he stood and walked over to me. "Of course."

Wrapping his arms around me, he gave me a gentle kiss and led me over to my bed. As I knelt down, he sat beside me and started running his fingers through my hair.

"I need you to tell me if I'm doing something wrong or if there's something you need me to do—something specific."

Nodding, because I wasn't sure my voice would work, I settled back on my legs and set the gear on the floor. I watched Jackson sort through the things I'd brought him, and the first thing he picked up was my collar. His fingers caressed the leather, and he looked at it like it was precious and important.

"I've been looking at collars online. I'm probably not supposed to mention that yet, but there's such a variety out there, and I want to get you both collars that represent you." Jackson looked up at me and brought it up to my neck.

It felt almost the same as when Cooper put the collar around me, but something about the way Jackson did it felt different. It was probably nothing, or maybe it was just the significance I was placing on it. But my master was putting a collar on me.

As he buckled it around my neck, I felt his fingers caress along the edges and watched his intense gaze focus on me. It was like there was nothing in the room but us, even though I knew Cooper was watching quietly from the corner.

I expected Jackson to pick up my gloves or my kneepads, since I'd just brought out everything, but he simply ran his hands over my face and hair and down over my neck again. I wasn't sure if he was going slow because he was worried about me, or because it was important to him, but there was no rush either way.

His touch gradually changed from careful to commanding as we both grew more comfortable. When he finally picked up the gloves and slipped them over my hands, I was relaxed and sliding into that place where nothing else mattered. Jackson continued to touch and caress me in long soothing strokes, eventually moving to my tail.

He moved close when he picked up the lube. Leaning against him, I closed my eyes and relaxed into him. Even the sound of the cap and the feel of his fingers circling my opening couldn't push away the fog and its calm that was sinking over me.

He took his time stretching me and readying me for the plug. By the time he inserted my tail, everything seemed very far away, and all I could focus on was the peace that flowed through me.

When I was ready, I opened my eyes and saw Cooper lying right beside me. I could see love in his eyes, and I knew if I looked up I'd see it mirrored in Jackson's. Cooper gave a little bark and his tail wagged. I peeked up at Master and saw his tender gaze focused on me.

He started to speak, and the words seemed like they were coming from a distance. But I forced myself to focus on what he was saying and not try to hide from him. "My two sweet pups. You are beautiful."

Master's hands reached out and caressed both of us. I simply leaned into his touch and closed my eyes, but I could hear Cooper dancing around excitedly. Master laughed. "All right, boy. Go play. Bring your ball, and I'll throw it for you."

Maybe next time I would run through the tunnel and over the fences, but at that moment, all I wanted to do was curl up with Master. I heard Cooper bounce away, and Master brought both hands and wrapped them around me. "Come here, sweet boy. I know what you want."

I didn't even open my eyes. I just curled up beside him and let my head rest on his leg. Master continued the soothing caresses down my back, along my legs, before circling up toward my neck again. Occasionally he would nudge my tail, or his hand would slide under and caress my belly. But mostly, his touch was sweet and almost innocent.

Everything was simpler as a pup. There were no worries. There were no fears. All I had to focus on was the warmth of my master, the sound of Cooper playing, and the knowledge that Master was in charge. Curled up next to Master, everything faded away, and I couldn't remember why I'd fought against this for so long. It was perfect.

15

JACKSON

"This is getting ridiculous." Wrapping my arms around Cooper, I pulled him back to the bed. "You stay here and use my car, and Sawyer can use yours. Then you both come back here tonight. There's no reason for you to leave this early and go back to the apartment unless that's what you want."

Cooper giggled. "You just don't want to have to get up yet."

"Damn right." We were still trying to figure out a good schedule, but Mondays always seemed to be the hardest. In the two weeks since they'd met my parents for the first time, Cooper and Sawyer had begun staying over more, but organizing three people and two cars was difficult.

Especially when they felt bad about borrowing mine. "Just because he has to go in entirely too early doesn't mean we have to get up."

I picked my head up and opened my eyes long enough to wink at Sawyer who was standing by the bed, shaking his head. "If you come back here tonight, we can do something together before Cooper comes home."

"I don't mind, but Cooper might have other plans, and I know we need to do laundry." Sawyer started digging through the dresser and grabbing clothes for the day.

"I told you that you needed to leave more stuff here." Tightening my arms around Cooper, I pinned him to the bed. "You don't want to go, do you? You want to stay here and sleep and cuddle with me, don't you?"

Cooper giggled. "I could be bribed. Are you going to make pancakes later?"

"Hey! Why does he get pancakes?" Sawyer looked offended.

Laughing, I looked over at him again. "Because you don't really like them. You have leftovers nearly every morning."

"That's not the point." Sawyer huffed and started heading for the bathroom.

Cooper snorted. "That is the point, nut."

"We'll do something fun together, I promise. How about we make something new for dinner?" I started thinking of recipes. "Maybe something that neither of us has tried before."

I'd gone to the grocery store earlier in the week, so I had a pretty stocked cabinet. "Give me a call at lunch and see if we need you to stop and grab something on the way home. But we should be fine."

Sawyer sighed, but it was more for effect and drama. "I guess that'll work, but I may need additional bribery."

Grinning, I heard Sawyer shut the bathroom door. "Of course, I'm sure you can think of something."

He grumbled about having to function when we got to sleep in, but I just rolled to my side and pulled Cooper into my arms, so his face was pressed against my chest. "Go back to sleep. You don't have to be at work until after lunch. My alarm is set to go off in another two hours."

Cooper mumbled something that sounded like an agreement and took a deep breath, relaxing into me. He was out in seconds. I stayed awake longer, listening to Sawyer get ready and blowing him a kiss as he finally left the bedroom.

I don't remember falling asleep again, but eventually, my alarm started blaring, and I rolled away from the warmth of Cooper's body to turn off the noise. When he opened his eyes for the second time that morning, he actually looked awake.

"Did we decide that we were sleeping here again tonight?" Cooper's face scrunched up in confusion. "I don't remember what we said, but I know we talked about it this morning."

"Yes." Nodding, I lay back down on the bed and gave him a kiss. "You're going to take my car when you go to work because I don't need it today. Then you'll both come back here tonight. You said you were working late because you were going to be going over more of the management stuff. Was that right?"

"I hope I'm not wasting my time." Cooper sat up enough that I could wrap my arms around him and pull him into my lap. He laughed and laid his head on my shoulder. "Once school starts in a few weeks, I won't have time to stay later, so I need to get all the additional training done now, even though they might not pick a manager for months. Maybe longer."

I turned my head, so I could kiss his cheek. "They would be stupid to pick somebody else. You're going back to school to get your degree. You're a hard worker and a dedicated employee. And most importantly, you're great with people and you understand the business."

"But what if they give it to somebody else?" His voice sounded small and concerned.

"Like what is the worst-case scenario?" I wasn't sure if he wanted someone to listen to his fears or someone to help him actually plan out what might happen. I was good with either, but I needed more information.

"Yes, what if I don't get the position until I finish my degree?" Cooper sighed.

"Then you still have lots of options. We figure out how to help you get your degree faster, or we look at different companies with other career paths. You're smart, you deal well with people, and you've got a lot of time to find the right option if this isn't it." I wasn't sure if I helped or made things worse.

"You won't think I failed?" Cooper lifted his head up and gave me a questioning look.

"Of course not. It took me years to figure out what I wanted to do. You might decide to switch majors twice, and it might take you a while to figure out the right career, but you have time." Giving him another kiss, I brought my hand up to cup his cheek. "I am already so proud of everything you've accomplished and how you both went from having nothing to having a great apartment and two solid careers."

Cooper leaned into my touch smiled. "And I have to admit sometimes I forget how much older you are than me. Those extra few years kind of give you an advantage in the career department."

I laughed. "Just a few extra years."

Cooper moved to straddle my lap. "You know that doesn't matter. I think you're perfect. I can't imagine having a master who's our age and just as unsettled as we are. I like that you know what you want in your career and that you're old enough to be so confident."

"I'm glad that the age difference doesn't bother you. It's not something I've ever noticed before, but I know that for some people it would be surprising." And I liked taking care of them, even though I knew they could do it themselves. They'd proved to be more than capable of succeeding. I just wanted to give them a boost and to be there to cheer them on.

Cooper grinned. "Your mother thinks you're robbing the cradle."

"I don't think you were supposed to hear that part." We'd gotten a good scare last weekend when my mother showed up unexpectedly. Luckily, Cooper had remembered to lock the doors, and we'd had all our clothes on. But it'd taken us entirely too long to remember that we'd still had the dog beds in the living room.

She'd stopped by after running some errands to see if we wanted a birdfeeder that my father had been convinced Cooper would love. He'd *oohed* and *ahhed* over it and had been so excited that she teased me about robbing the cradle as she was hugging me good-bye.

"I'm just glad they liked us." Cooper glanced at the clock. "I'm hungry. When am I going to get my pancakes?"

I shrugged. "I knew they would love you." He gave me a look like he'd understood what I hadn't said. "And I can't make you pancakes until you get off my lap."

Cooper wiggled his bottom on my growing erection. "I don't know what I want more."

I gave his ass a smack and shook my head. "You want breakfast, because I know how sore you are."

Cooper pouted. "But—"

"No buts. We made love twice yesterday, and you had your tail in for a long time." Giving him a tender smile, I kissed him gently. "Maybe if you're good, I'll help you wash up in the shower."

That was tempting enough to get Cooper scrambling off

the bed. "What kind of pancakes are we going to make? Oh, how about the chocolate chip ones you made last weekend? Those were great."

He looked so eager. "There is no way I'm sending you to work on a sugar high. We both know how much caffeine and sugar you're going to consume this afternoon."

"That's no fun."

Grinning, I climbed off the bed. "How about we do blueberry pancakes? And I think I have some sausage we can cook."

Cooper's grin returned. "That sounds great." He started hurrying toward the bathroom, but then he stopped and looked back. "When are we going back to the good pancake restaurant again?"

"We can go anytime you want. Do you want to go there for breakfast or dinner?" As I waited for his answer, I walked over to the dresser and grabbed a pair of pants.

"Dinner!"

Somehow, I expected that. "Then we will work out a time with Sawyer for us to have a date. Because I don't think he's going to want pancakes for dinner."

"Probably not." Cooper laughed as he closed the door. His voice called out, "Maybe we could have an early dinner next weekend, and then I can stop by and learn how to do some of the woodworking stuff with your dad while you do something with Sawyer."

I thought that sounded so boring it would be painful, but he seemed excited. "That sounds like a good plan. I'll call my parents this week and see what their weekend looks like."

Heading toward the bedroom door, I spoke up to make sure he could hear me. "I'm going to get the coffee started. I'll meet you in the kitchen. Remember, no funny business."

A giggle escaped the bathroom. "I'll be good."

Stopping by the hall bathroom, I did my business and went to the kitchen. Cooper followed quickly behind me, so I knew he'd behaved. They'd both done a very good job of following the rules, but I was still waiting for someone to actually ask permission.

So far, Cooper was the only one who'd even hinted that he wanted permission. But he really just wanted to be told no. Sawyer, on the other hand, would only ask when he actually wanted something.

Cooper bounced around the kitchen while I finished getting the coffee ready. He was getting flour and random things out for the pancakes. The combinations were interesting. Finally, I decided to start giving him directions, and by the time I was pouring two mugs of coffee, he had the pancakes started.

Part of me hated that Sawyer wasn't here to see how funny he was, but I also liked that Cooper and I got to spend time together. There was also another part of me that was looking forward to having a quiet evening with Sawyer. So I had to remember that everything balanced out in the end.

BY THE TIME I'D FINISHED UP WITH MY LAST CLASS FOR the evening, Sawyer was already home. "How was your work today?"

Sawyer shrugged, looking a little distracted. "Not bad. A little monotonous—but that will change later in the week when we get a new contract. It's for the landscaping in a planned community on the other side of town. It's more upscale and they want a different look to it, so we'll be able to do something outside the box, which is always fun."

Giving him a quick kiss, I pulled him into my arms. "I smell funny, so I'm going to go get a shower, but when I'm done, we can start making dinner if you're hungry."

Sawyer pretended to sniff me and frown, but the laughter in his eyes ruined it. "Yes, I think a shower is in order."

Considering I'd had puppies climbing all over me today and a very large German shepherd who kept rubbing up against me, he was lucky I didn't smell worse. "Why don't you come back and talk to me while I get a shower?"

"Just talk?"

"I plan on taking my time with you later, not rushing in the shower." Giving him another quick kiss, I stepped back. "Why, did you have different plans?"

Sawyer shook his head, smiling. "Taking your time sounds like a good idea."

As we walked back into the house, I started stripping off my clothes. I was naked before I reached the bathroom. Turning on the shower, I looked back to Sawyer, who was eyeing me and letting me know he enjoyed the view.

"I think it would be a good idea if I started looking to hire somebody. I can do the classes and the paperwork on my own, but when I start adding in the cleanup and things like that, it makes a long day. When it was just me, I didn't mind working as much, but with you guys here, I don't want to work until all hours of the night."

Sawyer was nodding, but I could see there was something going through his brain. "What?"

He shrugged but answered. "With as much time as we spend over here, any employee would realize we weren't just friends."

I nodded as I got in the shower. "I understand that. I would have to make sure that I hired someone open-minded, someone who wouldn't be offended by any part of my life. But I'm okay with not hiding the fact that I'm seeing you guys and that we're more than just friends."

Sawyer was quiet as I grabbed the shampoo. When I was rinsing it out, and he still hadn't responded, I poked my head of the curtain. "Does that bother you?"

He looked deep in thought, but not upset. Finally, he shook his head. "No, it doesn't really bother me. It's just going so fast, I guess."

He must've seen something on my face, because he shook his head. "Not *bad* fast...it's just weird."

"I know what you mean about this feeling fast, but I like where this is going. I like having you guys here. I like doing things with you. I like being able to take you to meet my family, and I don't mind the idea of introducing you to friends or employees." Working so many hours, and such odd ones from everybody else, I'd let friendships fade away. So there really weren't that many people to introduce him to.

"I used to go out and do things with friends, but I let myself get wrapped up in working a ridiculous number of hours a week and didn't make an effort to respond to people." Grabbing the soap, I went back to scrubbing.

I could hear a smile in Sawyer's voice. "I think I'm grateful for that. If you would've had a more normal social life and real friends, you might never have responded to our email."

"That would've been tragic." I stuck my head out of the shower again and gave him a smile. "Responding back to you was the smartest thing I've ever done."

As I finished getting cleaned up, I turned the water off. Sawyer was there with a towel and a tempting grin on his face. I wasn't going to be swayed. Drying off, I made us both settle for a kiss and a quick smack on his bottom.

Getting dressed quickly, I had us back in the kitchen within minutes. As we started getting everything out, I went back to our previous discussion. "You never really said how you felt about us telling more people. I know how serious I am with this, and I know how serious you both are. That's not a question in my mind. But I just need to know how you see things progressing. I don't want to rush you."

Sawyer set down the rice that he gotten out of the cabinet and walked over to wrap his arms around me. "I guess I'm a little bit worried about the ramifications of people finding out. This isn't casual for me, and I know it's not for Cooper either, but it's a big step."

And that answered my question, but I wasn't sure if he realized that or not. "So you need more time? I can put off hiring somebody for a little while. But that might mean I need to work more hours again because some things are falling behind."

Sawyer let his head rest on my shoulder, and I felt him relaxing on me. "I realize that 'I don't know' is a terrible answer. I'm just not sure what to say."

"Then we wait." I tightened my arms around him and gave him a hug. "And in the meantime, I might drag you into cleanup duty, especially when the puppies have their class. That took forever."

Sawyer laughed. "It's a deal."

The fact that he hadn't said no meant a lot to me. Everything in our relationship was happening faster than he expected, but I knew he would get there in his own time. Finding the right balance between being patient for Sawyer and not letting Cooper push us too fast was hard. But the more we talked, the easier it became to work through things and to get Sawyer to open up.

I was probably greedy. Him showing me his pup was such a huge step, but seeing that proof of how he felt, and how he was opening up, only made me want more. Yep, I was greedy. But I wasn't going to apologize for that; I was just going to remind myself what I had in my arms and where we would be, eventually.

16

COOPER

"Why are we over here? I mean, I understand that we live here, but why are we here and not at the house?" Watching Sawyer on the couch, flicking channels, I knew my question was going to drive him crazy, but I couldn't help it.

Sawyer shrugged but wouldn't look at me. Focusing across the room, I flopped down beside him on the couch. When it was clear I wasn't going to be ignored, he glanced at me. "We live here."

"*Duh.*"

Frowning, Sawyer went back to looking at the TV. "He needs some time away from us once in a while. He had to work late, so we'd be over there for hours without him. There's probably something wrong with that. It's not our house."

"We are fabulous, and nobody needs time away from us." Then I started to think about what he said. "Do you need time away from me?"

Was that he was trying to hint at?

Sawyer immediately turned back to me and pulled me into his arms. "No, absolutely not. I love you. We're family. I don't need time apart from you."

"But Jackson loves us. Why would he want time away from us?" That statement usually made Sawyer crazy, but he just curled into me and shrugged.

That was weird.

"Why do you think he wants time away from us?" Sawyer had been acting weird all night.

He'd been acting weird for a couple of days, really. Monday night, he'd been a little quiet but nothing too bad. But Tuesday morning when we got ready for the day, he'd said that we should probably go back to the apartment.

Now I was starting to think he didn't know what he wanted.

"He should." I could feel the stress Sawyer's body and hear in his voice.

"Are you ready to tell me what's bothering you?" I thought he realized it was obvious, but the way he stiffened made it seem as though he was surprised. "What happened on Monday?"

I knew he and Jackson hadn't argued—neither one was a volatile type, and neither was the kind of person who would hide it. It had to have been something with work or maybe something random. I couldn't think of anything a stranger would say or do that would make him this…odd.

Sawyer was quiet for a moment, then spoke quietly. "My boss wants to have a company barbecue. He's doing it over at one of the big parks on the other side of town, so there will be play equipment for kids and plenty of space to run around."

At first glance, that shouldn't be stressful. But I had a feeling I knew what the problem was. Waiting for Sawyer to tell me, I stayed quiet and just held him. When he finally realized I wasn't going to say anything, he sighed and continued. "He wants it to be a family event. Everyone will be bringing their spouses and kids. I don't know what to do. They know I'm gay, and I've never hidden you. But it makes me uncomfortable, and then there's Jackson. I don't want to leave him out of it, because he feels like family. But I don't know if they're going to lose their marbles if I show up with both of you."

"We knew this was going to happen, eventually." Sure, in the past when we talked about finding a third, it'd seemed far away. But we knew this day would come.

"I know, but what happens if we bring him and I lose my job? What happens if we don't bring him and he's hurt? What happens if we don't bring him and we accidentally bring him up in conversation? It's basically lying not to bring him. He's family too." Sawyer didn't seem to realize that, but I thought he'd already answered his own questions.

Giving him a quick kiss, I tried to think of how to respond. "If he's family, why are we having this conversation without him?"

I thought that was the most important question, but I kept going anyway. "If it's lying, and we know we'll want to talk about him, then I think you already know what we should do....But I'm not sure what will happen."

I wasn't going to claim to know everything, or that it wouldn't be difficult. "I don't know if they'll understand or they'll be horrified. But I do know that no matter what job you have next week, we will still have Jackson in our life. A week from now, a month from now, years from now, I'm confident he's going to be there. Are you?"

Sawyer had grown more still as I continued to speak,

and by the time I was done, I wasn't sure he was breathing. Giving him a chance to think it over, I resisted the urge to poke him for an answer or to tease him into smiling. This was one of those times that I knew it would be fine, but he had to work through it on his own.

When he finally started to speak, his words were hesitant. "Yes, but it's scary." He took a deep breath and continued, his voice getting stronger. "I should've talked about this with him yesterday. It was all just mixed up in my head....And I really don't know why we're here."

Sawyer sat up and looked around the room. "I like it when we're over at Jackson's."

"He calls it home when he's talking about it, even when he's talking to us." I had to smile. I liked it when he did that. "He cleared drawers in the dresser for us and even took some of his clothes over to the guest room closet so we would have more space."

Sawyer smiled, and his hold on me relaxed into something gentler. "And he rearranged everything in the bathroom to make sure we would have a place to put our stuff."

"And he buys things at the grocery store for all of us. He even gets food he doesn't really like." That still made me laugh; Jackson did not understand the draw of sweet breakfast cereal.

Sawyer nodded. I understood that Jackson was trying to show us he was ready for something more, but I wasn't sure if Sawyer had let himself see that yet. Jackson had done it in a lot of little ways lately.

He rearranged his schedule to make sure I could use the car on nights that I worked late. He made sure to spend quality time with each of us without making the other feel left out. I caught him the other day trying to figure out where to put an office for me, so I'd be able to study at his house. Jackson was tired of us going back to the apartment.

"He seemed kind of sad when I said we were coming back to the apartment tonight." Sawyer looked like he was starting to feel guilty.

"He would've understood if you said you wanted time where it was just the two of us. He's been really good about that. But you talked about laundry and paying bills and chores. That's not the same." I wasn't going to give Sawyer any more of a guilt trip than he was already giving himself, but Jackson's feelings had been hurt.

I had texted him on and off most of the day, and I knew he was feeling better. He was still very confused, though. I think in his mind, he'd done something wrong. "Do you really think he wants us there that much? Like, all the time?"

"I think what you're trying to ask is, 'Do you think he wants us to live with him?' "

Duh.

Sawyer nodded hesitantly. "Yes."

"Yes, I think he does." And I think he's wanted it for a while. He'd probably thought it was too soon to bring it up.

Sawyer seemed to be able to read my mind. "But isn't it too soon?"

"Why?" I gave Sawyer a long look. "We're two submissives who like being puppies. I don't see why we should go by somebody else's schedule. Two boring people in a very boring relationship might need a while to figure out what they want, but we are anything but boring."

Sawyer finally smiled. "I cannot argue with that."

"Because you know I'm right." Giving him a long, lingering kiss, I tried to show him how much I loved him and how much confidence I had. I knew everything would work out. When he finally pulled away, I gave him a soft smile. "How about we go find Master and tell him what's going on at work?"

Sawyer nodded slowly. "We can discuss the possible outcomes with him and see what he thinks. At the very least, he's part of the family, and he needs a chance to voice his opinion."

"And then we can talk to him about the living arrangements?" Jackson's house felt like a home.

"You're sure about that?" He seemed hesitant but not afraid.

I wasn't sure exactly what he was talking about. "What do you mean?"

"Well, are you sure you want to live with him? And I guess, are you sure that that's what he wants?" Sawyer looked away. "I don't want to get that part wrong. I don't want to push him into something he's not ready for and overwhelm him."

Without me, these two would never end up living together. "I'm positive. He keeps trying to give you a key, and the other day he was talking about changing one of the guestrooms around, so it could be an office for me. He wanted me to have the space to do homework, so I wouldn't have to come back here to do it."

If Jackson had been any more obvious, he'd have gotten it tattooed on his forehead.

But Sawyer wasn't going to relax until he heard it for himself. In his mind, people eventually sent you away or left. For some reason, I was never included in that list, but it was going to take a while until Jackson was included too. Jackson didn't seem to mind, though; he understood that Sawyer didn't have the easiest time growing up.

Finally, Sawyer nodded. "Let's grab some clothes and head over to Jackson's house."

I lifted one eyebrow. "Head over to whose house?"

Sawyer laughed. "Jackson's house for now. Maybe our house at some point."

I just rolled my eyes. "Like next week."

Climbing off the couch, Sawyer shook his head. "I will never be as confident as you are about some things."

I hopped up and followed him into the bedroom. "That's what you have me for."

What would he do without me?

WORRY WAS CLEAR ON JACKSON'S FACE WHEN HE opened the door. "Is everything okay?"

Nodding, I jumped into his arms. "We missed you."

Sawyer chuckled. "And we had something we wanted to talk to you about."

I gave Jackson a grin and stuck my tongue out at Sawyer. "Two somethings we wanted to talk to you about."

Jackson started to relax, but he still looked curious and slightly concerned. "Well, tell me your 'somethings.'"

Setting me down, Jackson let us inside. "Come on, you guys. Have you eaten?"

Sawyer and I both nodded. I batted my eyelashes at Jackson and gave him a little grin. "But is there any ice cream left?"

Jackson laughed. "So that's the real reason you came over, huh? You just wanted dessert."

"You found me out." Grabbing Sawyer's hand, I marched us to the kitchen. "Did you eat all the chocolate while we were gone?"

Jackson shrugged and grinned. "Quite possibly. You left me alone for far too long with chocolate in the house."

"Hey! The chocolate was mine." He picked out

strawberry at the store, so my ice cream had better be waiting for me.

See, this was why we all needed to live in one place.

This was much better. Jackson was here; my puppy bed was here; my ice cream was here, and this was where we needed to be. Releasing Sawyer once he was in the kitchen and couldn't escape very easily, I started digging around in the freezer. "Here it is!"

Since I was having some, everyone else felt justified in joining me. When we were finally all settled at the table, ice cream in hand, Jackson started asking more questions. "I'm glad you're back. I like it when you're at home. But I thought you were going to spend the night at the apartment?"

"Well, we were." I shrugged and shoved another bite of ice cream in my mouth. When I swallowed, I started again. "Sawyer had something he wanted to talk to you about, and so did I. So we decided to come home."

Sawyer stiffened, but Jackson nodded like it made perfect sense. Because to him, it did. This was home. Jackson glanced over to Sawyer. "What's on your mind?"

Sawyer sighed and started poking at his ice cream. A waste of chocolate if you asked me. "I should've talked to you about this last night, but I chickened out. My boss is having a company picnic next week, and he wants everyone to bring their families. Well, you're family, but I don't know what will happen if I show up with both of you."

Jackson was quiet for just a moment. "Is it something we have to figure out tonight, or do we have time to think things over?"

Sawyer shrugged. "He's assuming that everybody will show up with one partner unless they have kids, so he's looking for a rough headcount, but me adding one more

166

person isn't going to matter. It's hamburgers and things like that."

Jackson looked relieved. "Then let's take our time over the next couple of days and think about our options. I'm going to say this right off the bat, though. I don't mind staying home and not going if it makes things easier for you at work. I know having two partners would be more than a lot of people could handle."

Swallowing his bite, Sawyer shook his head. "But that feels like lying. You're as big a part of my family as Cooper is."

Jackson smiled and leaned over the table to give Sawyer a kiss. "Thank you for that. But my staying home doesn't mean…" Jackson's voice trailed off a moment before he continued. "But my staying home doesn't mean I'm unimportant or that you're ashamed of me. Our personal life is nobody else's business. Especially when you're at work."

"But we don't have to figure it out tonight?" Sawyer continued to poke at his ice cream as I finished mine.

Jackson shook his head. "No, we have plenty of time."

Sawyer seemed to relax at Jackson's confidence. But there was no saving his ice cream. It was a soupy mess. Standing up, I shook my head. "Next time, no ice cream for you if you're just going to waste it."

They both laughed as I started clearing up the bowls. When the kitchen was clean again, Jackson gave us both kisses and pulled us close. "How about we go lie down in bed and finish this conversation there?"

I nodded enthusiastically. I was hoping the next part of our conversation would lead to kissing and fun stuff. Sawyer, on the other hand, was still nervous, so I was the one who responded for both of us. "Yes."

Jackson smiled but held Sawyer close as we went to the

bedroom. Jackson seemed to understand that Sawyer was uncomfortable about something, because he kept his clothes on as he climbed onto the bed and held out his arms. "Come here, you two."

Sawyer slowly joined Jackson, but I jumped onto the mattress and threw myself down beside him. When I was on one side and Sawyer on the other, I reached across and grabbed his hand. Jackson was patient as we settled in, but I knew he was starting to reach his limit. "So who's going to tell me what else we have to discuss?"

I loved the way he didn't immediately jump to conclusions or assume something was wrong, even though we showed up right before bed acting very strangely. Sawyer didn't seem like he was ready to open up, so I figured it was my turn again. "Do you want us to move in?"

Jackson chuckled, but Sawyer started coughing like he'd choked on his own tongue. When Sawyer could breathe, I looked back at Jackson expectantly. "Well?"

I thought it was a simple question.

Jackson looked at both of us, clearly not sure how to answer. "I don't want to make either of you nervous. I'm going to be patient."

I didn't bother trying to hide my sigh as I rolled my eyes. "We're just going to pretend he doesn't look like he's going to barf. So if we both looked functional, what would you say?"

"Cooper!" Sawyer seemed to disagree with my description.

"You really do look green." Smiling at Jackson, I raised one eyebrow. "Remember, we are pretending everyone's functional."

Jackson didn't seem like he could pretend that well, but he answered anyway. "I like having both of you around. I think of this as your home too. I'm not going to justify how soon it's been or make things sound simpler. But if we boil everything down to just what I want, I'd rather you be here."

He took a deep breath, and when neither of us panicked, he continued. "So, yes, I'd like it if you moved in."

I gave Jackson a big kiss and then turned to Sawyer and smirked. "See, I told you so!"

17

SAWYER

"That's not helpful at all." Jackson gave Cooper's ass a smack. Which was probably what the brat had been aiming for.

It had broken the tension, though.

"Are you sure?" Okay, that was probably a stupid question. "I mean, I don't want you to say something because you think that's what we want to hear."

Jackson's smile was tender as he looked at me. "Sweetheart, you really do look like you're going to vomit. I promise, I'm not saying what I think you want to hear." Then his smile widened as he looked at Cooper. "This little nut, on the other hand, is very clear about what he wants."

That made me laugh. "A spanking?"

"That too." Jackson leaned close and gave me a kiss. "I was very serious when I said I wasn't going to rush you."

I nodded, I knew that. I also knew that I might fight what I wanted forever. "I'm not saying that I'm completely comfortable, because you wouldn't believe it. But I think of this place as home. After work sometimes, I find myself making the turn to come here, even when I'm supposed to be heading back to the apartment. I like knowing that I'm going to see you at night. I like curling up with you and watching TV when Cooper's at work. You're part of our family, and family is supposed to be together."

Saying it that way made it easier for my nerves to settle. It was just that simple. Family was supposed to be together. Jackson seemed to believe me, because I felt the tension leak out of him and the worry on his face seemed to fade.

When Jackson spoke again, I could hear his confidence surging. "Then I guess it's decided. Now we just need to look at your lease and the practical side of things."

"Tonight?" Cooper didn't seem excited about the planning part.

Jackson gave him a look that said he wasn't buying the act. "Why, did you have something else in mind?"

"Yes!" Cooper pressed closer into Jackson's side, rubbing his cock against Jackson's thigh. "Do you need a hint?"

Jackson chuckled but looked at me. "What do you think? Should we plan, or do you think we should go with Cooper's idea? He looks like he's been naughty, so I'm not sure if we should reward him."

I knew he was trying to give me a chance to take things in a different direction, but I was ready to stop thinking. I wanted to sink into both of them and let everything else fade away. "Unfortunately, I have to say he's been good."

Cooper gave both of us a wicked grin. "I've been *very* good."

"Then I guess I'll just have to let you have your way." Then Jackson's smile turned wicked. "But I know exactly what I want."

The need and arousal in his voice sent shivers down my spine. But the look on his face had my cock jerking.

Jackson's hand started moving over my back and down

to my ass. "I bet you just want to relax and make everything go away."

Nodding, I leaned in and pressed a kiss to his lips. That was exactly what I wanted. Jackson's hand squeezed my cheek and his gaze grew heated. "I want you to sit up, so we can strip you."

Cooper made an excited little noise and sat up, pulling at my clothes. "You're not going fast enough. I'll help."

Jackson watched as Cooper enthusiastically bared me. "I want you to lie down in the middle of the bed. I have a surprise for you."

As he climbed off the bed, I followed instructions. I wasn't sure what he was going to do, but the look on his face said he was going to enjoy it. Jackson walked into the closet and came out quickly, holding something in his hands. "Face down on the bed, Sawyer. Stretch out so your arms are at the headboard."

Cooper understood what was happening before I did. He made a low pleasured noise and I could picture him giving Jackson the sweetest looks. "Can I play with it next time?"

Jackson made a low rumbling sound, and I picture him nodding. "If you're very good."

Cooper seemed to be willing to promise anything if he got to play. But I still wasn't sure what Jackson was holding. "I'll be very good. I promise."

"Then help me get Sawyer ready." I wasn't sure if that sounded ominous or sexy.

I squeezed my eyes shut as I felt the bed move, not sure if I should peek or not. Jackson's warm hands started rubbing long strokes down my back, and it was impossible not to relax into his touch. "That's better. I want you nice and calm."

It wasn't long before I felt Cooper's hands rubbing over

me as well. Soothing me seemed to be their primary goal, but the combination of their hands wandering over me and the excitement about what was to come made it erotic as well.

When Jackson stretched my hands above my head, I didn't even think about where it was going. The feeling of something wrapping around my wrists and his deep voice called me back from the fog I was sinking into. "When we were talking about limits, Sawyer, you said you liked being tied down."

I wasn't sure if it was a question or not, but Cooper handled it anyway. "Yes, Master, he loves being restrained."

Jackson knew that I had my safeword, so he continued to wrap the soft, lined cuffs around my wrists. I felt the bed shift, and Jackson reached for something at the head of the bed. He must've put some kind of chain or hook there, because my hands were quickly tied down.

My face was still pressed against the mattress, my eyes closed, but soon I felt Cooper's hands bringing something around my eyes. Some kind of scarf wrapped around my face, and the combination pushed me deeper into that soothing place where nothing mattered. Restrained and blindfolded, there was nothing I could do but let Jackson take control.

As I relaxed into the bed, I felt their hands start to move again. Jackson's rougher ones started at my shoulders while Cooper's long, soft fingers started at my feet. I might've felt guilty about being the center of attention and getting all of their focus, but there was nothing I could do, and nothing was up to me.

There was no guilt in submission.

The room was quiet; the only sounds were their breathing and the low noises that seemed to flow out of me. Hands moved my legs to spread them apart, and the massage continued everywhere. I wasn't sure if I was supposed to push against the arousal that was building or not, but it was fighting the hazy feeling that was trying to pull me down. The combination kept me aware but relaxed and calm but aroused.

When I felt the first touch of a lubed finger against my ass, arousal surged to the surface. "Shh," Jackson's low voice made me want to squirm and beg. "I'm not in any rush. You're just going to relax for me."

I wasn't sure if it was supposed to be a reward or punishment.

One finger slowly eased inside me, and I felt my body open around it. The rest of the hands moved away, and all I was left with was that one touch. Somehow going from an almost endless number of hands to one point on my body just magnified it.

I expected the rhythm to change, but he never varied from that carefully measured pace. When I could feel his knuckles against my skin, he started gently easing out of me. Part of me wanted to soak it up, and part of me wanted to move and demand more.

But what I wanted most of all was whatever Jackson wanted to give me.

We continued the slow, torturous pleasure for what felt like hours. When a second finger entered me, they felt huge even though I knew it wasn't enough of a stretch. It took me several minutes to figure out it was Jackson and Cooper in me at the same time.

The feelings that rushed through me were overwhelming. When the third entered me, it didn't matter whose finger it was. I knew they were both there loving and touching me. When I was finally empty, I expected to be filled or fucked or something, but Jackson's voice pulled me away from the wonderful sensations that were flooding me.

"All right Cooper. Help me roll him over. There's so much left of his body that we haven't massaged." Jackson seemed to realize that my muscles wouldn't work, because I felt the restraints release my arms and they moved me without my having to do anything.

I felt both sets of hands massage my arms before they were stretched up again and restrained the top of the bed. When they had me laid out once again, the massage started over. Cooper was on my chest, and I felt Jackson's hands on my legs. He worked his way up my calves and thighs slowly and methodically.

Cooper's touch seemed designed to arouse and not relax. He focused on my nipples and seemed to take great pleasure in teasing and pulling at them. As Jackson finally reached the top of my thighs, I felt him move my legs apart again.

I should have been thrusting up against him or begging for more, but nothing seemed to work. Shivers raced through me, and I could hear needy sounds escaping, but they seemed out of my control.

His gentle touch took forever to reach the tops of my thighs. When all the hands were removed from my body, I knew what was going to happen. The feeling of Jackson's fingers as they wrapped around my dick tore a moan from me. It was like my ass all over again, the one incredible sensation after the long overwhelming pleasure.

I knew I couldn't come. No matter how long the silence lasted or how incredible his touch, I had to wait for permission. But the need kept building...the tight, smooth strokes up and down my cock...the light, caress of his thumb over the head...it just kept building until I knew I was begging for something, but the words didn't make sense.

When Jackson released my dick, I cried out. I heard

soothing noises coming from the darkness, but it was the feeling of his hands lifting my legs that let me know he wasn't going to stop. My knees were pushed up until my thighs rested against my chest and I was spread open for him. Then I felt Cooper's hands again, holding a leg with one, and the other sliding down to open my ass.

To offer it up for Master.

Just the thought had my already hard erection jerking, and it was all I could do to hold back the pleasure. I felt Jackson's body stretch out over me, and his cock barely kissed the tip of my hole. He slid in deep with one quick thrust that had fireworks shooting up my spine.

After the long slow pleasure, I expected more of the same, so the spike of need and the beat of arousal as he fucked me deep had me moaning and crying out. They released my legs and let me wrap them around his waist, to try to pull him closer. The feeling of Cooper's hand on my hard length and his lips on my nipple pushed me even higher.

Sensations were flooding through me and all I could do was let go and offer everything up to Jackson. As he thrust deep inside of me, hitting that spot that made lightning shoot up through me, I finally heard him begin to speak.

The low words made me want to reach out to him in the darkness. "That's my beautiful Sawyer, giving everything up to us. That's what you want isn't it, my beautiful boy? You want to give everything up to your master like you've given it up to Cooper."

The tender words stroked deep inside me. "Please. Yes."

"I want it all, my beautiful boy, my sweet pup, my loving, wonderful Sawyer. There's nothing you need to hide from me. No desire too wild, no love too deep, nothing you need to hold back. I promise, I'm strong enough to catch you and steady enough to be here no matter what."

I felt the fabric slip over my head, and for one long moment, I kept my eyes shut, wanting to hold back the whirl of emotions. When I finally opened them, I was staring at my two perfect loves. Cooper, my family, my partner, and my rock…and Jackson…my master, my lover, and the rock who would be there for both of us.

As the pleasure threatened to break over me, Cooper moved to lie beside me and Jackson leaned down to kiss me. It was sweet and tender, and I felt tears prickling in my eyes. The soft touch of Cooper's lips against my cheek pushed me over. One small little caress that was innocent and perfect.

A dam of emotion burst through me. My orgasm was beating down on me, and I cried out, pleading to come. Jackson's beautiful words and honest emotion had tears and pleasure exploding at once. "I love you, Sawyer. Show me how much you love me. I know you do. Show me how much."

My orgasm rushed through me in waves, each one higher than the rest. Cooper sprinkled kisses on my face and Jackson kept thrusting deeper and pushing me higher until everything shattered, and I was carried away on the pleasure.

I could feel my orgasm finally fading, but it was far away. I was floating above everything, and all I had to do was let the incredible rush take me away. Jackson came, and I wanted to reach up and touch him, to make him feel as good as I did, but my hands wouldn't work.

I closed my eyes as he pulled out, sighing as he wrapped himself around me. I was surrounded by the two people I loved the most. I could hear Cooper and Jackson exchanging soft words, and I knew Cooper had finally told him. Cooper held so much love inside of him, and watching him hold it back because I wasn't ready had been almost painful.

Knowing that he was finally free lifted a weight off me that I hadn't realized was there. As I floated away, everything perfect and calm for the first time in so long, I found the words for one moment before the blackness pulled me down. "I love you, Jackson."

18

JACKSON

"This is getting ridiculous." Cooper's whispered words had me looking up from the area I was straightening.

Cooper looked frustrated, but Sawyer looked guilty. It made me wonder what they'd been up to. In the days since we'd talked about moving in together, they'd spent a lot of time at my house. While I was starting to see that having a big house had been a good idea, I also loved having them around. I just wished I didn't have to work such long hours.

Between classes and lessons and just general business crap, not to mention cleaning real puppy crap, I'd had several long days in a row. The guys had said that they didn't mind, but it looked like they'd been up to something and finally wanted to confess.

Was it terrible that I thought they looked cute?

"I thought you guys were going to pick out dinner? Is everything okay? I'm almost done." They'd come out earlier to ask what they could do to help, but they'd already worked their full-time jobs, and I felt bad asking them to do more, so they'd offered to make dinner.

Cooper smiled. "We put a casserole in the oven. There's

a recipe grid online where you just pick out one option from each box and then you have dinner. It looks like it's going to turn out good."

Sawyer nodded, but the guilt hadn't faded. Not sure if he was ready to talk about it or not, I gave him a teasing grin. "I'm going to need a shower after I'm done. I might need someone to help me wash my back."

Normally, they would have argued, or at least teased, about who got to help me. But this time, Cooper elbowed Sawyer and gave him another frustrated look. Sawyer finally spoke up. "I honestly didn't realize how many hours you were putting in here. I've been thinking about the conversation we had about you wanting to hire somebody, and I feel bad."

I jumped in. "No, don't feel bad about being honest. I've been doing the same schedule for several years, and I just wanted to have more time for you. I don't mind the actual hours."

Cooper piped up. "But you deserve more time to relax, and you shouldn't have to do everything."

"Cooper and I were talking, and I think I found an option that I'm kind of comfortable with...maybe comfortable." Sawyer shrugged and looked like he was talking about a dentist appointment, not a possible employee.

Over the last couple of days, Sawyer had grown more confident. But the look on his face made me think we were backpedaling. Feeling loved and hearing the words had left him relaxed, but I didn't like the look on his face. Setting down the toys, I walked over to the door.

"I won't touch you because I'm gross. But I still want kisses." That finally brought a smile from Sawyer. After two quick kisses, I gave him a long look. "We do things at our own pace. You weren't ready to have people know about us. There's nothing wrong with that."

Sawyer interrupted. "You're right, and if it were someone else or a different situation, I might not have said anything. Having people know is scary, but we've gone over all the possible outcomes, and I think this is a step I can handle."

Now he had me curious.

We'd spent the last couple of days talking about the practical side of the moving in and the what-if scenarios around both of their employers possibly finding out about our life. We'd even gone over the financials of the business, so I could show them that even if it declined, we could still eat and pay the bills.

"Tell me about your step." I leaned in and gave him another kiss. "Next time, you have to wait to tell me until I'm clean enough to hug you."

They both laughed, and Sawyer shook his head. "Yesterday when I went in my boss's office, his daughter was walking out. They had some kind of fight, and it looked like he wanted to talk. Well, it turned out that she, and I'm not sure if that's the right pronoun, is having a hard time finding a job because she's non-binary, I think. He didn't say it that way, but by the words he used and the awkward way he said tomboy makes me think he doesn't understand. In his mind, she should just pretend to be more feminine to get a job."

Now I was the one shaking my head. "That's terrible. Telling them that everything would be better if they just lied isn't helpful. There are websites for everything these days. He needs to look this shit up."

Sawyer nodded. "Well, she's just out of high school, and it doesn't sound like she has any real skills, at least according to him, but I thought it might be worth talking to her. No matter how she identifies, I knew you wouldn't have an issue with it, and let's face it, if she gets feeling different, she might understand us more." Then he frowned again. "And that's a little bit selfish."

"It's honest and practical, and we're allowed to be selfish when it comes to our own life and privacy." I'd been thinking along the same lines, so I wasn't going to let him beat himself up. "I would've wanted to hire somebody who could relate on some level, so I think it's a good idea."

Cooper was growing impatient, and he seemed to think we were both morons, so I kept going. "Why don't you get her number, and I'll talk to her. Do you know if she's expecting a phone call, or is this going to come out of the blue?"

Sawyer reached into his pocket and pulled out a piece of paper. "This has her information on it. I'm really not sure though—about the pronouns. If I'd met her in a social situation, I probably would've assumed male pronouns or asked. He said her name is Amanda, but yeah, I have no idea what she wants to be called."

"It sounds like he has no idea how to discuss this stuff with her. And yeah, I'm going to have to be careful and not assume pronouns. Did he say he was going to talk to her?" I was already trying to figure out how to start the conversation without sounding weird or creepy, and it was hard.

"Yes, he said he was going to talk to her when he got home." Sawyer seemed to be feeling less guilty now—his posture was more relaxed and his smile more open.

"Okay then, I'll give her a call as soon as I clean up." I looked around at the room. "I'm almost done here for the time being. I need somebody to remind me to go through my email tonight. It's been a couple of days since I did that."

Cooper shook his head. "I'll go through the email. I'll let you know if there's anything important. Then after dinner, we're going to sit down and look at everything that needs to be done and figure out how to divide it up better if, whatever the person wants to be called, doesn't actually end up being hired."

I opened my mouth to speak, but Cooper just kept going. "I know you said we already had jobs, but we would rather help and have time with you in the evening than sit around watching TV and not spend time with you. So you're not going to argue."

Part of me wanted to push back against what he was saying, but the more sensible piece said he was right. And it also reminded me that he wasn't just my boyfriend; we were a family and had to make decisions together. "I can live with that for now, but once we find someone we're comfortable with, then you guys go back to having one job."

With Cooper going to school, he was going to have two jobs for a while anyway, and that would make it harder on everyone. He didn't need to be helping me on top of everything else. "Okay, five minutes here, and then I'll come inside."

Cooper gave me a look that said he had a better idea. "One or two minutes, because Sawyer is going to help, and I'll go inside and get the emails done. By the time you get back to the house and get a shower, dinner will be ready. After we eat, you can give them a call."

Smiling, I nodded. "That sounds like a plan. Thank you for your help."

I leaned in and gave Cooper a kiss. As he started to leave, Sawyer called out, "Don't you need to get his computer password or something to answer those emails?"

Cooper laughed. "He doesn't even lock doors. There's

no way his computer has a password, and he probably has his email login automatically saved in his computer."

I wanted to be able to say I was more careful, but I didn't want to lie. "Um, sorry?"

Sawyer was shaking his head like he couldn't believe it. "We are going to have a discussion about you being more careful."

"I'll do my best?" Promising to remember would be a lie, but they were right. "How about I say thanks for helping me, and we ignore the fact that I'm an idiot?"

Sawyer laughed. "I'll do my best."

"WELL, THAT HAD TO BE THE MOST AWKWARD EMPLOYEE interview ever." Flopping back on the couch, I yawned.

Not only hadn't her father mentioned his conversation with Sawyer, I wasn't sure she'd ever had anyone ask what pronouns she wanted used. At first, she seemed to think I was teasing, and for a few seconds, I'd worried that Sawyer had read the signs wrong. But after a few minutes, she opened up and admitted that yes, female pronouns were fine, but she wanted to be called Lee, her middle name.

She'd been very honest about the fact that she would not wear skirts and pretend to be ladylike just because it made customers happy. When I told her I didn't care—as long as she was dressed and polite to my customers and their dogs—she didn't seem to believe me.

Looking over at Sawyer, I frowned. "Are you sure about this? She's not the meek type who's going to sit back and just wonder why we're so accepting. She's going to ask questions and figure it out."

Sawyer had been sitting at the other end of the couch, but as he started to speak, he moved closer and ended up curled up next to me. "Yes, I understand. I like what I'm doing, and I can see working at the company for years. But eventually, more about my personal life is going to come out. I need to know if this is going to cause a problem, so I can start looking at other options."

Wrapping my arms around him, I pressed a kiss to his head. "Worst-case scenario, we know everything will work out. Right?"

Sighing, Sawyer nodded. "But I don't want to be some unemployed slob who just mooches off you and Cooper."

I had to laugh. "I cannot picture that at all. But even if you do end up unemployed for a little while, I know you'll figure something else out. Besides, just because we planned for the worst doesn't mean that that will happen."

Cooper sat up from where he was lying on the floor and grinned. "You can always be the little house boy who runs around naked. That would be hot."

"Oh yes, that would be hot." I trailed my fingers down Sawyer's side. "I think you would be a fabulous naked houseboy."

He laughed and rolled over, so his head was on my lap and he was staring up at me. "Not a chance."

Cooper sighed like Sawyer just didn't understand. "I think we should put it to a vote."

I nodded. "I like that idea."

Sawyer snorted. "When is she coming over for an interview?"

Evidently, he didn't like the idea of being our naked little sex slave. "Tomorrow around dinner, after the lessons are done for the day and Cooper's back."

Sawyer seemed lost in thought, but I wanted to finish the conversation. "As long as the regular part of the interview is fine, I'd like to introduce both of you to her before I officially hire her. I think I'll know pretty quickly if she's open-minded enough for it to work out. Right now, all she knows is that I'm a friend. If we've read things wrong and she wouldn't be a good fit, then we'll just leave it at that."

Cooper's expression made it clear he thought it was the best option. But we both waited to see how Sawyer felt. He was quiet for several minutes. I couldn't tell if he was thinking it through logically, or just worrying.

By the time he was ready to speak, Cooper and I were both nervous. "I think that's the best idea. If we lie about it now and she turns out to be a great employee, then she'll be pissed we didn't tell her the truth. You need help. There's no way around that. And something about her just feels right."

I had to agree. "Once we got through the initial weird part, she came across like she would be a hard worker and wouldn't give me a lot of bullshit. She's expecting to stand out, but I think once she realizes that this could be a place where she fits in, I think it'll really work out."

"I agree." Cooper's big smile and pure excitement were contagious. "Then we know it will be perfect." Cooper leaned in close and gave me a kiss. "Are you guys still going to have time to grab a load from the apartment this weekend?"

They still had over a month until their lease ended, so we were planning to go every couple of days to bring back a load. Their furniture was going to go in storage until we figured out what to do with it. But we were going to handle that last.

Cooper had to work most of the day on Saturday, so the plan was for Sawyer and me to make a run to the apartment midafternoon. Nodding, I mentally ran through the schedule one more time. "It should still be fine. Depending on how quickly I get cleaned up, we might even be able to do two loads."

Cooper grinned. "Perfect, then I'll have more of my clothes here, and I won't have to do a dozen loads of laundry a week."

Sawyer took offense to that. "Hey, I've done the last three loads of laundry."

I shrugged. "See, all the more reason to keep you both naked."

Excitement ran through Cooper. "I'll be your naked houseboy. If you get a pool, I'll even wear one of those tiny little suits and be your naughty pool boy."

Sawyer snickered. "He should have gone into porn, not coffee. We'd have been millionaires by now."

"But then you'd have been too famous, because everyone would have loved him, and I wouldn't have met you." No matter what he did, I knew Cooper would succeed. People loved his openness and the teasing way he flirted with just about everyone.

Cooper threw himself across my lap, nearly smothering Sawyer. "I wouldn't trade that for all the money in the world."

The sincerity in his voice was at odds with the crazy words, but I understood the sentiment. "I love you both. Now let Sawyer breathe."

I would have smiled, but it wasn't the most insane thing I'd said that day. Life with my guys would never be boring.

19

COOPER

I was over-caffeinated; that was my only excuse. Well, maybe justification…or explanation. Yes, I liked that better. It was my explanation. Caffeine, sugar, chocolate, and excitement were a bad combination.

As more of our stuff started moving from the apartment to the house, it made everything more real, and more wonderful. When I thought about how wonderful it was, my excitement kept growing, and somehow that led to more coffee consumption. I still wasn't sure how that happened.

By the end of my shift, I'd had three, no four, oh, maybe more than that….Yes, too much caffeine. It made the day pass by faster, but it also seemed to turn my brain off. As I was dancing around the storeroom, getting ready to leave, April finally came in demanding answers.

"You've been bouncing around the store since I came in. And according to everybody else, you've been doing it all morning. I even had one of the customers a few minutes ago say that they thought you'd had too much caffeine. So spill it." She crossed her arms over her chest and leaned back against the door. "What? Did Sawyer ask you to marry him? If you were a girl, I'd ask if you were pregnant. You're glowing, and you're stupid excited."

Oops.

I had no idea what to say. "We're getting a new place?"

Unfortunately, that came out as a question, which didn't help my situation.

April gave me a suspicious look. "Why?"

"Because we need more room?" Shit, a question again.

"I know neither of you are pregnant. So unless you just got married and are trying to adopt a baby from some third world country, I don't see why you need a bigger place. Your apartment is cute." Her face went from frustrated to concerned. "Are you guys having money issues? Did you get kicked out? No, that doesn't explain the excitement."

"No, everything's fine." Everything was perfect.

"What the hell is going on? I thought I was your friend, but you're lying about something. If you don't want to tell me, that's fine." As her tone changed to hurt, I was even more conflicted.

She was right. She was my friend. But there was a huge part of my life that I'd left out.

After telling Sawyer that I approved of whatever decision he made about his job, I'd done my best to ignore the fact that I had the same decision looming. "It's personal. I don't mind sharing with my friend. But I'm not sure it's something my boss needs to know."

I finally sat down on one of the chairs and tried to pretend I was calm. "Can you see my dilemma?"

April nodded, but she didn't look pleased. "I thought you knew me better than that. As long as it honestly doesn't affect your work, it's not my business as your manager. As a friend, you can tell me anything."

I had a feeling I was going to test that "anything" to the limit.

Deciding to just go for it, I blurted it out. "Sawyer and I are moving in with Jackson. He's our third. We met him online. We're in love."

I was pretty pleased that I'd managed to leave the puppy stuff and the BDSM out of it completely.

April's eyes widened. "You guys are in an open relationship?"

I shook my head. "No, it's just the three of us. We're all committed to each other, and we're tired of going back and forth between his house and the apartment."

"Is this new?" She wasn't running away screaming, but she still seemed confused.

I wasn't sure what she was talking about. "Well, we've always known we wanted a third. If that's what you mean. But we met Jackson a few weeks ago. Things just grew from there."

"Wow." The frustration had faded, and it looked like the confusion was starting to clear. "That's great. You seem really excited. I can't wait to meet him. This explains why you guys haven't invited me over for dinner lately."

I winced at that. "We haven't really told anybody besides his family. I honestly wasn't sure if it would freak you out."

April nodded, finally seeming to understand. "I guess I get it. You're going to get a lot of shit from some people. But honestly, this isn't the weirdest thing I've heard from a friend."

"Yeah, I just don't want it to keep me from moving up in the company. I like my job." Then I gave her a little pout to lighten the mood and make her laugh. "And I want the manager job at the new location."

She smiled but didn't get sidetracked. "Eventually, one of the other managers or employees will ask you about your family—there's no way around that. But I honestly can't remember having a personal conversation with anyone at the corporate office."

I could see her starting to think back through previous conversations, and finally, she shook her head. "No, I don't remember anybody asking me if I was even married, except that lady in HR. As long as you hire people who are open-minded and fit in with the overall feeling of the company, I don't see where you'll have a problem."

"Great, that's a load off my shoulders." Standing up, I started patting myself down to make sure I had my keys and phone. "I have to go help unload the car, because they were going over to the apartment to get a load of stuff."

"When am I going to meet this fabulous guy who's got you so excited?" April grinned.

I shrugged. "Why don't you come over for dinner next week? Let me talk with the guys and see what works best for everybody's schedule."

Beaming, April nodded. "Perfect. I get free food and entertainment."

Laughing, I shook my head. "You'd better behave."

"I make no promises." She shrugged. "I said the same thing when I met Sawyer for the first time. Remember?"

"Well, this will be just as G-rated." Nodding, I made a vow to make sure everything weird was picked up and put away.

"If I'm going to live vicariously through you, it needs to be at least PG." She smirked and stepped away from the door. "Okay, go home to your men. You'll have more fun than I will tonight."

I gave her a little wink as I turned the handle. "I know." Her laughter followed me out the door.

"I can't see anything. Can you?" Pressing my face harder against the window, I kept trying to see what was happening over at the other building.

When Lee had pulled into the parking lot over by the training center, Jackson had gone out to meet her. Sawyer and I had waited in the house, watching as they talked in the driveway. They both looked stiff and slightly uncomfortable, but as they kept going, their body language changed.

Lee's hands came out of her pockets, and Jackson laughed. We were too far away to hear what they'd said, but things looked like they were going well. When they finally went into the building, Sawyer and I stayed glued to the window.

Deciding that he needed a distraction, and probably because I was still too over-caffeinated, I started telling him about work. "I might have accidentally told people about us."

Sawyer groaned. "What part about us?"

I giggled. "Not the good stuff."

He gave me a frustrated look. "That doesn't tell me enough."

"Just that we're moving in with Jackson. Nothing about the puppy play, or the spankings, or the BDSM, or the fact that his sister writes dirty books." I thought, overall, I'd done pretty good.

Sawyer snorted. "I guess when you put it that way, us just living with a third doesn't seem so weird."

"Nope, that's what I thought." I leaned over and gave him a kiss. "April wants to know when she can meet him."

Laughing, Sawyer started to relax. "She's going to love him."

"Because he's so hot and perfect. It's going to drive her

crazy to be single when I have two sexy men." And I was going to enjoy every minute of it.

Before Sawyer could respond, his phone went off. It was Jackson.

"What does it say?" I leaned over his shoulder trying to look at it.

"Just be patient." I ignored his short tone because I knew we were both excited.

"That's not going to happen." He finally angled the screen so I could see. "That's not enough information."

Sawyer nodded. "I guess we'll find out when we get there."

Sending us a short text that just said to come out to the work building was not sufficient. In seconds, we were out the back door and heading over to the work side of the property. As we got closer, I could feel the tension in the air.

"He wouldn't even have us come down if he didn't like her." I reached for his hand and gave it a squeeze. "So at least we know you have good instincts about employees."

Sawyer gave a small bark of laughter, but it didn't sound funny. "What if she thinks we're weird?"

"We are weird." I gave him a look that said it was a stupid question.

"Okay, what if she's shocked and horrified and tells everybody at my work?" He was sweet when he was nervous, but I gave him another "You're a moron" look.

"We've had this discussion. I love you. Jackson loves you. Even if you get fired tomorrow, nobody will starve, and nothing bad will happen. Hell, even if we both get fired tomorrow, nothing bad will happen. Jackson won't be angry or disappointed. We'll be able to figure it all out."

I loved being able to say that. No matter what happened, we could deal with it.

"Now if we're unemployed for a long time, Jackson's going to make us start cleaning the house naked. There's no way around that." I gave Sawyer a wink and released his hand as we got to the door. "Are you ready?"

He smiled, looking a little calmer. "Yes."

The door opened, and Jackson was standing there looking very pleased and relaxed. "Come on in. I have someone I want to introduce you to." Lee was standing there, looking slightly awkward, with her hands folded across her chest. She was dressed in jeans and a plaid button-down, and with her short hair, she did have a very gender-neutral look. But overall, she was really cute, and I had a feeling the customers would like her once she relaxed.

When we were watching them talk, she seemed friendly and open. I wasn't sure what they'd discussed, but now she was clearly concerned.

Smiling, I waved. "Hi, I'm Cooper."

"Hi, I'm Sawyer. We met briefly the other day." Sawyer looked just as awkward as she did.

Jackson shook his head at them both. "Lee is going to be working with me part-time. To start, she's going to be here a few afternoons a week, and then she'll help out with the classes on Saturday. I explained that I was looking for someone open-minded, because my living arrangements were not traditional."

I rolled my eyes. "She's going to think you're insane or doing something weird."

Lee was now giving him a suspicious look. I liked her. She was smart. Jackson didn't seem to mind her skepticism; he just ignored us both and continued. "Lee, I would like you to meet my boyfriends, Sawyer and Cooper. We're keeping our life fairly quiet, but because you're going to be here so often, I didn't want to lie to you."

She thawed a little, but I had a feeling it would take her

a while to get used to all of us. She glanced at the three of us, then gave a slow nod. "Nice to meet you. I'm Lee. I'll trade you one awkward question for another. Yes, girl pronouns for now, but I don't know about later. So what's the deal with all three of you—you're really boyfriends?"

Sawyer wasn't sure what to say, so I took this one. "If you ever want us to start using different pronouns, just say so. And yes, we're together, but kind of in the closet, sort of. At least with the fact that there are three of us."

"Yeah, my dad mentioned that Sawyer had a long-term partner." She glanced at Jackson. "He said you were a friend of theirs."

Sawyer finally spoke up. "Because work doesn't know. I plan on telling him this week before the barbecue."

She rolled her eyes. "He's stupid about some things, but I don't think you have anything to worry about—if that's what you're thinking. Dad is one of those clueless open-minded people. He'll probably say something offensive, eventually, but he won't understand why it was wrong."

It was clear that he'd aimed some of his stupid remarks at her.

Sawyer shrugged. "As long as I don't get fired, and he doesn't get too weird, I'm good with a few stupid remarks."

Jackson didn't look like he was fine with that idea, but he held his tongue. I had a feeling we would hear about it later, though. Turning to Jackson, I tried to break the tension that was beginning to grow again. "So when does she start?"

"Monday." Jackson looked relieved to be able to say that. "She's going to be learning where everything is and watching some of the classes. Then once she's up to speed, she's going to help with some of the office stuff as well. She's got school in just a few weeks, but we should be able to work around her schedule."

"That's great." Jackson would get more time off, and it would make everything easier. Maybe even dates on a regular basis and more sleep for him. We hadn't realized what crazy hours he'd been working until we moved in with him. He would take time off when we were around but would then work insane hours when we were gone — neither of which was good long-term.

Overall, I thought it was going to work out great.

And even though it wasn't my business, it looked like Lee needed a place where she could be herself. So I had a feeling it was going to work out for her as well.

20

SAWYER

The room was dark, so I knew it was too early to get up, but my brain wouldn't listen. Refusing to give in and open my eyes, I rolled over and snuggled deeper into Jackson's embrace. Sometimes I felt trapped between the two of them, but today, it was perfect.

I wanted to go back to sleep, but my mind kept going over everything that had happened and obsessing over the future. Telling my boss hadn't gone as badly as I expected. He'd been surprised, but as his daughter had predicted, it wasn't a problem. But the next hurdle was going to be showing up at the barbecue and letting everyone else see our family.

It would be awkward, but I knew it would be fine. Or at least, that was what I kept telling myself. I was hoping if I said it enough, Cooper's belief would start rubbing off on me. So far it wasn't working.

Whispered words came from Jackson. "Your mind is a very loud place this morning."

I hadn't meant to wake anyone else up. "Sorry."

I felt him press a kiss to my hair. "Are you okay?"

"Yes, just nervous."

Jackson didn't offer to stay home again; once I'd made up my mind, he'd done his best to support me even though my worries made him uneasy. He would have done anything to make it easier on me, but this was something that wasn't really under his control.

His arms tightened around me, and I felt his hands start rubbing up and down my back. The long slow strokes eventually put me back to sleep, but Cooper took that moment to roll over, and his hard length pressed against my thigh.

At first, I wasn't sure if he was asleep, but when his hands started moving down my sides to cup my ass, I knew he was awake. When his fingers teased over my crack and I moaned, he giggled. Jackson sighed, but I could hear the smile in his voice.

"You are both up way too early. We were supposed to be able to sleep in today." He was right; that was supposed to be the point. Cooper had even taken Sunday off to make sure he would be able to go to the barbecue. We were supposed to have had a lazy morning doing absolutely nothing.

Evidently, my brain hadn't gotten the memo.

Cooper was itching for attention. His hips rocked against me again and I felt fingers start teasing around my hole. "Master, Cooper's being naughty."

Pleasure rumbled deep in Jackson, and his husky voice sent a shiver down my spine. "What's my naughty boy doing?"

"He's touching my ass and teasing my hole. He's trying to get me to disobey too, but I remember the rule." I gasped when I felt Cooper's teeth on my shoulder. "He's being very naughty, Master. He's licking me and…his teeth…"

How was I supposed to think when he was doing that with his finger?

Jackson chuckled, and I felt him start to move. I heard a smack, and a moan echoed in the room as Cooper soaked up the pleasure from the spanking. "He is being bad this morning."

"You're going to have to punish him." I wasn't in the mood for a spanking, but it was clear that Cooper was antsy for something a little rougher.

"I think you're right, Sawyer. I think I need to remind this naughty boy who he belongs to." Cooper finally stilled, and I wasn't sure what Jackson did, but another cry of pleasure rolled through the room. "I have just the thing."

Jackson rolled out of bed. Curious to see what he was up to, I opened one eye and watched his beautiful body walk across the room. Jackson had enjoyed going through the toys that we'd accumulated, so when he walked over to the box on the dresser that had his favorites, I wasn't surprised.

"Sawyer, I want you to roll over and get Cooper nice and hard for me." Jackson's voice made my cock jerk. We were both too excited to even think about questioning him. Cooper thrust his dick into my hand as soon as I reached back for him.

He let out another low moan as I wrapped my fingers around his erection. He must have been having a fabulous dream, because he was hard, and I could even feel precum starting to drip from his slit.

As Jackson came back to the bed, he climbed up from the bottom of the mattress and got between us. "That's right, I want him as hard as you can get him."

Sleep must have been still fogging my brain. As he held out the strip of leather, I wasn't sure what it was for the longest time. Cooper gasped as he figured it out first, but my brain wasn't far behind him. The new cock ring.

The strip of leather buckled around his cock almost like a collar for his dick. As Jackson slid the covers off, baring us both, I felt Cooper jerk in my hand. He wanted it. I let go of his cock long enough to roll over, then I went back to stroking him while Master watched. Whispering in Cooper's ear, I watched the pleasure on Jackson's face. "Master's going to tighten that around your dick because you were naughty. He's going to use you for his pleasure, but you might not get to come at all. That's what happens when you're naughty, Cooper."

Cooper moaned and thrust his hips up to grind his cock harder against my hand. He was going to come if I kept it up. Jackson must have seen that too, because he shook his head. "Let him go. It's not time for him to come."

As I pulled my hand away from his length, Jackson took my hand and moved it up, responding. "Why don't you play with his nipples for a while?"

"Thank you, Master." Leaning down to Cooper's chest, I took one nub into my mouth and let my hand slide over to the other and start teasing it.

I watched as Jackson wrapped the leather around Cooper's erection, trapping all the pleasures so he wouldn't be able to come. When Jackson was finished, he looked back at me. "A little bit rougher...I want them to be nice and sensitive later. Every time his shirt rubs across his chest, he's going to remember he was naughty."

Cooper's excited little whimper made it clear that wasn't a punishment. As Jackson spread out down the bed, so his mouth was hovering directly over Cooper's cock, I started sucking on his nipples harder and twisting them with my fingers.

Jackson let his tongue flick out and lick just the tip of

Cooper's dick. Cooper tried to thrust his body closer, but Jackson's hands moved to pin him to the bed. Jackson's low words had Cooper gasping, and I could feel a shiver run through him that time. "Naughty boys don't get to come, Cooper. Remember that."

I wasn't sure if he believed him or not, but Cooper seemed to love the threat. Jackson took Cooper's cock deep into his mouth before Cooper could even promise to behave. The sounds that poured out of Cooper were beautiful, and they made me work even harder.

There was no time to think about anything else. All I wanted to do was focus on Cooper and dragging more incredible noises out of him. I watched as Jackson licked and sucked and slowed him down. Cooper was moaning and pleading for more, but Jackson took his time making Cooper frantic with need.

When Jackson finally released his length, Cooper thought he was getting a break from the pleasure. He was gasping for breath, and his body sagged against the bed. But Jackson wasn't done with him yet. "Sawyer, hand me a pillow."

Quickly obeying, I watched as Master slid it under Cooper's ass. "Perfect." Jackson almost purred the words.

As he positioned his head even lower, he gave Cooper's hole the barest of licks before pulling back again. He ignored the gasp of pleasure that escaped from Cooper and gave me a wicked smile. "Now it's your turn to have a taste. Why don't you come play with his cock?"

Cooper groaned but just lay there soaking up the overload of sensations that had to be flooding through him. "Oh, I almost forgot."

Jackson seemed more excited than forgetful, so I knew the act was probably for Cooper's benefit. "I don't want those nubs to get lonely. Look what I found for them."

Jackson sat up enough so that the nipple clamps in his hands were visible. He held them up and gave them to me. "Put these on, then come back down and play with his cock."

Cooper's eyes were wide, and he was shaking with anticipation by the time I brought the clamps up to his chest. I'd always told him dirty stories about what our master would do to him, and these clamps had been a favorite. Right now, Cooper's brain had to be overloading as the fantasy was coming true.

The clamps were connected by a chain that stretched across his chest. Pleas and needy sounds were tumbling out of his body as Jackson started licking around his hole. When the first clamp went on, Jackson had to hold him down again because Cooper cried out and arched off the bed, the cock ring the only thing holding his orgasm back. When the second gripped his other nipple, Cooper started whimpering and writhing for more.

Jackson wasn't going to let Cooper set the pace though; he started exploring Cooper's tight hole again and directed me back to his cock. Every once in a while, Jackson would have me tug at the chain, or he'd stretch a hand up and flick absently at a clamped nipple while he fucked Cooper with his tongue.

Cooper cried out and begged and shook until all he did was moan. He sank into the bed, and I knew everything else had faded away—he was completely lost in the pleasure.

Jackson eventually asked for the lube and condoms from the drawer. Cooper gave another long moan, but he was too far gone to even beg for more. I watched as Jackson slowly lubed and stretched Cooper's needy hole, but when he reached up and had me move so he could start spreading the lube on Cooper's cock, I was confused.

"Now for you." Jackson's gaze had turned to focus on me, but I wasn't sure what he meant.

"Me?" I'd been hard since we'd started devouring Cooper, but that shouldn't have been enough to fry my brain too.

Jackson gave a low chuckle and nodded. "I want you to kneel over Cooper's cock. Don't sit back, though. It's your turn to be stretched."

That sounded more like a dirty, wonderful threat than a reward, but I wasn't going to complain. As I positioned myself over Cooper's body, he blinked up at me and made needy little sounds. Someone was ready to be fucked.

Jackson's slicked fingers started circling my hole, and he went through the same torturous process on me that he had on Cooper. By the time he entered me, I was ready to beg for more. As one finger became two, I was pleading for him to go faster, three fingers had me losing all focus and all I could do was hold myself up and let the pleasure run through me.

When he finally pulled out, I was shaking and my muscles felt like I'd run a marathon. Jackson's sexy words only pushed me higher, though. "That tight little hole is all ready. Show me how good it feels to have Cooper's cock sliding into you."

I could feel his hands wrapped around Cooper's cock to steady him, and that just made it even hotter. Cooper wasn't making love to me or even fucking me, Master was using Cooper's dick to fuck me. Cooper cried out in pleasure as I slowly sank onto him. The leather that was still wrapped around his erection kept me from taking him all the way inside me, but that little reminder about who Cooper's body belonged to...who we both belonged to...was the sexiest thing ever.

"Lean forward, Sawyer. That's right." Jackson

positioned me so Cooper's cock was just barely in my body. "Now, don't move."

Staring into Cooper's lust-filled eyes as Jackson moved me around was beautiful and erotic. I could feel Jackson shifting behind us and as Cooper's ass lifted a little more off the bed, I leaned down to kiss him.

Cooper's cry of pleasure echoed into the kiss as Jackson thrust into him. Incredible sensations rushed through me as Cooper's cock pushed into me. All I could do was wait for Jackson to give me the pleasure of Cooper's cock. It wasn't up to Cooper; it wasn't up to me. I just had to stay still, shaking and kissing Cooper as Jackson decided when to fuck Cooper hard enough to send his cock sliding into me.

It was maddening.

The feeling of being owned, the pleasure that rushed through me as Cooper's cock randomly nailed my prostate, the knowledge that everything was on display for Jackson and I was his to command...it was all too much...but it was never enough to come.

It was incredible.

Jackson kept us like that for minutes...hours...I couldn't be sure. Eventually, the only sounds in the room were the dirty noises from Jackson's cock and the whimpers of need from Cooper and me. When Jackson finally came, we were both frantic with desire, but neither of us wanted to upset Master or break the incredible tension and arousal that was building.

A whine broke out of me as Cooper's cock eased almost all the way out of my ass. I'd been so close. Jackson chuckled, and the wicked sound had both of us shivering. Cooper closed his eyes, and it was all I could do to keep from slamming my ass down on his dick.

When I felt Jackson's fingers trace around my hole, I gasped and tightened around Cooper's cock. "My good boys. Look at how sexy you are. I bet you're desperate to come."

It didn't seem to be a question, and I knew even if it was, answering would be almost impossible, so I just whined and tried to let him know how needy I was. Jackson's fingers must have caressed down Cooper's cock, because his eyes opened wide and he started to shake.

We were both so fucking close.

"How would you like to slide your cock deep inside my sexy boy, Sawyer? Would you like that?" The sexy promise in Jackson's voice forced the words out of me.

"Please...yes...please..." It wasn't much, but it was enough.

Jackson's hands wrapped around my hips, and he pulled me off Cooper's cock. "Show me how much you want him. Show me how good it feels to slide your dick deep inside him."

He positioned my shaking body between Cooper's legs and all I wanted to do was to sink into him, but I waited. "Can I...please...can..."

Fuck, my brain just wouldn't work.

"Do you want permission to come? Is that what you're asking?" It was clear Jackson knew exactly what I was doing, but he seemed to love pushing us both to the edge of sanity.

"Yes!"

"Then come." The words were all I needed to hear.

Thrusting deep into Cooper, I watched the pleasure on his face and I could feel his body clenching around me. I knew if I got his prostate just right I might be able to give him an orgasm, but I knew he wanted to feel the rush of cum as well.

"Please...Cooper...please..."

Jackson said something, but all I could focus on was

trying to wait until Cooper could come. When Jackson reached down and removed the restraint from around Cooper's erection, it only took one slow caress to push Cooper over the edge.

His body clamped down almost painfully around my cock, and my orgasm exploded through me. The rush of pleasure made me almost dizzy, and wave after wave of cum shot deep into Cooper as I thrust harder and harder, trying to keep the pleasure going.

When we were both spent and wrapped in a tangle of arms and legs on the bed, I felt Jackson's hands move over me slowly. Tender kisses were pressed against my head as he rolled me, so I was lying beside Cooper.

I was in and out as he climbed off the bed. A warm washcloth ran over my cock and around my still sensitive ass. Jackson gave a quiet laugh as I squirmed. Seconds later, Cooper made a low whine, and I felt him shiver too. When we were both clean enough to satisfy Jackson, the sheet came over us and he gave us matching kisses.

The last thing I remembered was soft words and his soothing touch as everything faded away.

21

JACKSON

"Do I need to say the words again?" Cooper sighed, and I could almost hear him rolling his eyes even though his face was turned away.

"No." Sawyer was starting to get frustrated, which was the only time he ever really got short with Cooper. "I'm fine."

"No, but everything is going to be fine. You just need to relax." When Cooper opened his mouth to continue the lecture, Sawyer broke in.

"Coop—"

Now it was my turn to interrupt. "If I have to turn this car around, there will be no spankings for a week."

That got their attention. Sawyer finally cracked a smile, and Cooper grinned. I could see the naughty wheels in his brain start to turn. Evidently, so could Sawyer.

"Dirty little slut." But Sawyer said it with a smile, and Cooper didn't seem offended. So I didn't worry.

Besides, we were almost there.

As we pulled into the parking lot, I could see people on the other side of the park underneath a pavilion. There didn't seem to be a sign, but I could tell from the way Sawyer watched them that it was his company. "We can still turn around. You can drop me off at home and then come back. You'll only be a few minutes late."

"I know." Sawyer reached for my hand. "I just have to remind myself that the hard part is done—this is just going to be awkward." Cooper and I had met Sawyer after work on Tuesday, he was so nervous about telling his boss after work, we hadn't wanted him to drive.

It ended up going fairly well. Lee was right; he was clueless, but not malicious. Sawyer was still so overwhelmed, though, that I was glad we'd gone to meet him. Sawyer was confident his job was not in jeopardy, but introducing us to the rest of the company was still awkward.

"We're fabulous! They're going to love us." Cooper's enthusiasm had Sawyer and me smiling, but I knew Sawyer wouldn't relax until the barbecue was over.

"Yes, we are." I tilted my head back, and Cooper leaned forward to give me a kiss.

"And besides, didn't Lee say she was going to be here?" Cooper started bouncing around the car looking out the windows. "She's really starting to open up."

Cooper was excited and nervous, but he was right. They were going to love us, and Lee was starting to open up. It was going to take a while for her to see that there were people out there that didn't care that she didn't follow traditional gender lines.

I think it helped that she could see there was something different about us. The other day Cooper had come in after work to say hi and give me a kiss, as he was excitedly telling about his day, she rolled her eyes and said he looked like some kind of little yappy dog. Cooper almost died laughing.

If she stayed around long enough, she was going to end

up figuring out the rest. She was too smart, and Cooper was too open for it not to happen. I didn't mind the idea, over time, and I'd grown to like the idea of having people in our lives we could talk to about it. Especially people I wasn't related to.

Cooper probably wouldn't care, but Sawyer would take time to get used to the idea. I just hoped that she wouldn't figure it out before he was ready. Lee's generation seemed to look at things very differently, though. Cooper and Sawyer still had more of the shyness about being different than I expected, but Lee didn't have that innate need to hide what made her unique. I found it fascinating.

After everything that had happened with their families, I guess I should have expected it. Most of the time, it looked like they'd moved on from the traumatic experiences that drove them both from their homes at such a young age. I had a feeling that they needed to talk about it all a lot more than they were letting on.

Before, Sawyer was too worried about sharing things with me and showing me who he really was inside for me to push too hard. The way things had changed for us lately and the trust he'd given me, I had to think that it was time for some deeper conversations. Mom always said that sharing things made the burden lighter.

Well, it was time for me to help take some of the weight he'd been carrying around.

"I think I see her over there. She's the one on the sidelines glaring daggers at the overdressed man in the suit." Cooper stopped his bouncing and gave the man a quizzical look. "Why is your boss wearing a suit to the park?"

"Why did he tell me the company embraced new romantic designs and supported my innovation?" Sawyer was serious, but Cooper still burst out laughing every time

Sawyer said it. Sawyer just rolled his eyes. "I'm not a fucking rocket ship."

I couldn't help it. "No, you're like one of those expensive self-driving cars." That had Cooper laughing so hard he was nearly on the floor.

Sawyer didn't seem to think Cooper was that funny. He opened his mouth to say something, but I reached over and took his hand. "You ready to go? Lee looks like she could use someone to keep her dad away."

Giving him someone else to focus on seemed to help. Sawyer nodded, "Her dad said the other day that he didn't understand people who made choices that were difficult but that he wasn't going to make things harder at work for anyone who was unique."

Cooper and I both rolled our eyes. Cooper flopped back against the seat. "He's a moron."

"Yup, he really doesn't get the difference between people who are making a lifestyle choice and what Lee is going through." Sawyer couldn't seem to understand it either. The more we learned about what Lee was dealing with at home, as well as her struggle to figure out who she was, the more respect I had for her.

Cooper said the other day that not killing her dad got her huge props from us. I'd had to laugh, but unfortunately, agree.

Sawyer sighed. "Let's go rescue her."

Taking a cue from him as he reached for the door handle, Cooper and I got out of the car as well. We all knew it was going to be awkward and stressful, but I thought it would be a good test run for how sharing our relationship with more people would go.

Which was just as scary as Sawyer was imagining...but there was a part of me that was ridiculously excited to be able to say that they were mine. As we walked across the grass field toward the crowd of people and the one clearly disgruntled girl that needed a family who understood her, I couldn't help but be proud of Sawyer.

He'd seen someone in need and had stepped out of his own comfort zone to help. Sawyer didn't always understand how incredible he was, but from the smile Cooper was giving him, I knew we could both see it, and I promised to find more ways to remind him.

As both boys flopped down on the couch, I had to smile at how different they were even when they were worn out from the stress of the day. Cooper was tired; I could see it in his eyes, but it was also clear he'd snuck too many desserts, because he was still bouncy and twitchy. Sawyer, on the other hand, looked like he'd been running a marathon and was exhausted but relieved it was finally over.

"How about we get you guys ready and you have some pup time?" Walking over to the couch, I leaned down to give them both kisses. Hopefully it would burn some of Cooper's excess energy so he could sleep tonight, and it would give Sawyer a chance to relax and process everything.

Both of my sweet boys nodded, and Cooper, of course, was the first to climb off the couch. "I'll go get the stuff."

"Thank you." As Cooper walked toward the bedroom, I turned to Sawyer. "I'll be right back. I have something I need to grab from the kitchen. You start getting undressed."

Sawyer nodded and sat up slowly. He wasn't going to win the race for who could get naked the fastest, but every time he showed me his pup, he seemed more comfortable and just happier overall.

M.A. INNES

Heading into the kitchen, I went over to the junk drawer and started digging through the odd items to the one important bag at the back. I'd had it in there for days, but I'd been worried that someone would find it first. Pulling out the little package, I felt a knot start to form, but I could feel the smile on my face. Sure, there was a part of me that was nervous, but I was fairly confident they would love them.

Sliding the two small surprises into my pocket, I went back out to the living room. Sawyer was naked and standing around like he was already lost in thought. Cooper, however, was sitting on the floor, spreading everything out, nearly bouncing with excitement.

"All right, let's get you ready." Trying to figure out how I wanted to do it, I thought for a second as I crossed the room and sat down on the floor. "Come here and kneel for me. I have a surprise for you."

Cooper's eyes widened, and he scampered around the gear to plop down beside me. "What is it?"

Smiling, I shook my head. "Just wait a minute."

He grinned at Sawyer. "Hurry. He won't show me until you come here."

Sawyer shook his head at Cooper's enthusiasm but started moving toward us. When he was kneeling on the other side of me, a questioning look on his face, I picked up their collars. "These aren't your final collars. We've discussed that. However, until we're ready for that, I thought these needed something to give them a little more personality."

Sawyer was watching me intently, but I could feel Cooper—he was so excited that he was nearly bouncing off the walls. Reaching into my pocket, I pulled out the name tags. "Okay, Cooper, you first, because I'm not sure you could wait even thirty more seconds."

Both boys nodded, and I could see laughter behind Sawyer's quiet expression. Picking up Cooper's collar, I started putting on the shiny tag. It was a silver metal with black writing, but it had an iridescent layer over it that gave it a rainbow effect when it caught the light.

"Cooper, you were the one who charged into life trying to figure out who you were and what you wanted. You didn't take the easy road, and you didn't hide from what made you special. You are my Maverick, my excitable pup who charges right in and isn't afraid of making waves." Giving him a tender kiss, I buckled the collar around his neck while he smiled and fought to contain his excitement until Sawyer got his as well.

When Cooper's collar was around his neck with the tag hanging down, I reached for Sawyer's. As I started to put his tag on the little metal ring, I smiled at him. "Sawyer, you took a chance on making a life with Cooper, then again when you found puppy play, and again when you guys talked about wanting a master...and the biggest chance of all was when you took one on me."

Pausing, I gave him a kiss as I watched emotion grow inside him and threaten to spill down his cheeks. "You are my Chance—because I want you to remember how strong you are and how proud I am of you."

As I brought the collar up to his neck, a shiver ran through him and the tears spilled over. Before I could wipe them away, Cooper leaned over and kissed them away. "That's the perfect name for you."

Sawyer didn't seem to know what to say. He looked slightly helpless and overwhelmed as I buckled the collar around his neck. Positioning his black tag with silver writing down his neck, I brought my hands up to cup his cheeks. "I love you. Sawyer...lover...pup...friend... Chance...every part of you."

Before Sawyer could respond, Cooper's enthusiasm bubbled over. "Let's go look. Come on. I have to see it in the mirror."

Taking Sawyer's hand and pulling him up, he half dragged and half carried the still slightly shocked Sawyer across the room. Laughing, Sawyer finally got caught up in Cooper's whirl of emotion. They ran back to the bathroom and I could hear them giggling and making excited noises.

Cooper's voice echoed from the bathroom. "Oh, look! It's got something on the back. Let me read yours."

I knew exactly what the back said:

Master's pup

As both my pups came running out of the bathroom, grins on their faces and love in their eyes, I couldn't help but feel my emotions wash over me. Finding my sweet pups might have been a complete accident, but I was their master by choice, and I couldn't think of anywhere else I would rather be.

ABOUT M.A. INNES

M.A. Innes is the pseudonym for best-selling author Shaw Montgomery. While Shaw writes femdom and m/m erotic romance. M.A. Innes is the side of Shaw that wants to write about topics that are more taboo. If you liked the book, please leave a short review. It is greatly appreciated.

Do you want to join the newsletter? Help with character names and get free sneak peeks at what's coming up? Just click on the link.

https://www.subscribepage.com/n1i5u1

You can also get information on upcoming books and ideas on Shaw's website.

www.authorshawmontgomery.com

ALSO BY M.A. INNES

AVAILABLE ON AUDIOBOOK

Secrets In The Dark
    Flawed Perfection
    Silent Strength
    Quiet Strength (Coming Spring 2018)

AVAILABLE ON AUDIOBOOK

Bound & Controlled Book 1: Garrett's story

Bound & Controlled Book 2: Brent's story

Bound & Controlled Book 3: Grant's story

Bound & Controlled Book 4: Bryce's story (Coming May 2018)

Bound & Controlled: The Complete Series (Coming June 2018)

UNEXPECTED

AN M/M AGE PLAY ROMANCE

"Who wants spinach and whole-wheat baby biscuits? The fruit-flavored or even vanilla ones are so much better." The male voice was familiar, maybe that's what drew my attention, but as the speaker continued, something had me stopping in the middle of the grocery aisle. "It's getting harder and harder to find the good ones. Organic green tea baby biscuits are not fun."

"Dude, you know that sounds so weird when you say shit like that." The new voice didn't seem surprised at the direction the conversation had taken, but I could almost hear the second young man shaking his head.

I could understand where he was coming from. Most people didn't go around talking about eating baby cookies —at least not in the grocery store.

The first voice didn't seem upset; in fact, the conversation had a familiar feel to it, like they'd had it before. "What? They're good, and I enjoy doing stuff that makes me feel like a kid again. It's like all those people who color and buy those fifty-dollar books and expensive crayons to help them relax. Same thing."

"Um, I think there's a bit of a difference between my mother coloring intricate designs in one of those stupid books and you eating baby cookies and watching cartoons." There was a pause, and I heard the cart moving around. "What brand of diapers did my mother send us here for?"

I should've kept going. That would've been the mature thing to do, the right thing. But no, I stood in the middle of the grocery store, trying to look like I was debating which paper towel roll to grab, while really listening to the most curious conversation I'd ever heard in public.

One voice was just so accepting and the other was so honest, I couldn't walk away.

"Those, no, not that one." The boy who liked the baby biscuits was clearly growing frustrated. "No, your sister is like the size of a bag of flour. Those diapers are way too big. No, not that brand, she's going to want the other."

"God, just grab what we were sent here for." It was clear that the second young man didn't find the baby aisle as interesting as the first.

"Okay, these." There was a short pause. "But wait, oh, they might have the good ones."

The good baby cookies or diapers?

Cookies.

"They put organic weird crap up at the top, but all the good ones down low. What are they trying to do, sell the junk food kind to babies in the carts?" There was quiet for a moment before he spoke again, and I could hear the excitement and almost triumph in his voice. "Yes, they've got the vanilla ones. Do you think my mother would notice if I came home with two bags?" There was a hopefulness in his voice that made me want to promise him all the cookies he could eat.

But the second voice was quick to burst his bubble.

"Yes. Your mother's nosy as hell. She'd end up thinking that you had a girl knocked up somewhere."

"Okay, I'll just grab one. But while we're here, I want to get some of those fruit squishy packs. She didn't think those were weird."

"Fruit squishy packs?" He reminded me of a frustrated parent who was trying to figure out what snack their toddler wanted.

It was interesting.

"You know...the applesauce in the pouches. I just told her it was to keep them from spilling in my backpack and that it was better for recycling. She said something about me doing a good job and thinking things through and just ignored it after that." He'd clearly gone to a lot of trouble just for applesauce.

"And we're just going to ignore the fact that it's weird you're picking out food designed for infants and toddlers, right?" I could hear the smile in the second boy's voice.

"Yup." The cheerful one didn't seem offended. "My parents are so excited for me to be an adult; I need every bit of fun I can get."

"Your parents have been this way for years." The second boy snorted, and I heard some movement from the cart. "You were the only kid in kindergarten in a suit."

The comment should have been teasing, but I had a feeling he was serious. The young man who was fond of cartoons and kids' snacks made an agreeing noise. "Yeah, but that little briefcase was awesome. They have no idea why I wanted to take a break this summer. They've had my future planned out since I could walk, and I think this is the last chance for me to forget about it all."

"You should just tell them you don't want to be an engineer." The second boy was clearly the more assertive up of the two.

The first young man snorted, clearly not fond of that idea. "And tell them I have no idea what I want to do, but being a kid again sounds like a good idea? No thanks."

I could understand exactly why he thought it sounded perfect, but I wasn't sure if he realized what he was saying or not. The second boy laughed. "They'd keel over from the shock."

The dry response made me fight back a laugh. "And I'd end up in prison for inducing a heart attack or something. I'm a hot bottom, but I don't have any desire to be some guy's bitch boy."

The second boy barked out a laugh. "Way to overshare in the grocery store, moron."

"There's no one here. Everyone in town is over at the fairgrounds or watching the game."

He was *almost* right.

The more confrontational of the two made a noise of agreement. "All you need is something crazy to get back to your parents right before they leave. Do you really think they'll cruise around Asia if they think you're having some kind of existential crisis?"

"Do you even know what that word means?" The interesting young man laughed.

And suddenly I knew exactly who he was...Ryland Owens.

The second voice had to belong to the young man I'd seen leaving the Owens' household several times. Ryland's friend was over there so often, I'd originally thought the family had two sons, not one.

Once I knew who was speaking, everything else clicked into place. Ryland was right. His parents treated him like an adult, but a coddled one who wasn't allowed too much freedom. I'd had dinner with them several times when he'd been in the dorms. I'd enjoyed it, but they were old enough that I didn't have much in common with them.

From what they'd said, Ryland was a surprise late-in-life baby that they hadn't planned on. Ryland's father was a doctor and his mother a high-powered lawyer, so I could only imagine what Ryland's childhood had been like.

"Come on, if we don't get back with the diapers my mother is going to kill me." Ryland's friend sighed dramatically.

"Your little sister's cute."

"You don't have to live with her or my mother going through her *oh shit I've got another baby* crisis."

"I still don't see how she can panic when it's what she wanted." Ryland honestly seemed confused, and it made me smile.

"Who knows—women are nuts." I couldn't decide if the friend's comment meant he liked women but didn't understand them or that he was gay too and had no interest in figuring them out.

"Amen."

Smiling wider, I heard their cart start to move. I should have walked in the other direction and pretended I hadn't heard them, but my feet started moving before my brain could make a more reasonable decision. Whispering to myself, I couldn't help but question what I was about to do. "A hyped-up sub on too much caffeine and sugar would have more sense. You're too old to do stupid things."

Evidently not.

I rounded the corner just in time to hear Ryland start speaking again. "Hey, do you remember those articles online where adults were using binkies to stop smoking and replace the sensation of having something in their mouths?" Without waiting for his companion to respond, he kept going. "These are not big enough for adults. Where do you think they found them?"

"Ry, dude, you—" Before he could finish what I was sure was going to be a severe scolding for saying something like that in the grocery store, he ran his cart into mine.

Perfect.

Looking back at me, the young man I'd seen with Ryland blinked at me. "Oh, sorry, man."

Giving him an understanding smile, I shrugged. "It's alright."

Then, before my brain could tell my mouth not to be stupid, I spoke again. "There are specialty websites for things like adult-sized binkies. They cater to a wide variety of lifestyles."

Yup, moron.

Ryland looked sweetly confused, like he'd been entirely too sheltered, but his friend's eyes widened until most of his face seemed to be big brown eyes and an open mouth. He knew exactly what I was talking about.

"Um, thanks." Ryland probably wouldn't have been so polite if he'd noticed the look on his friend's face, but his focus was entirely on me.

No impulse control. "You're welcome, boy."

Giving him a wink and a nod to his friend, I shifted my cart and kept going. Ryland said something low that sounded like a comment about their grocery list, but his friend couldn't seem to hold back his surprise.

"Dude, your neighbor is freaky." He said it fairly low, but in the almost silent store, it echoed down the aisle.

"What?" Without looking back, I wasn't sure what Ryland's expression was, but I had a feeling the confused, innocent look was back in full force.

"Ry, we really need to work on branching out your porn

habits." His friend sounded like a parent who had just about had enough. "Come on, we need to have a talk."

"About what?" That sweet, lost voice had my cock jerking.

"Ry..." Ryland's friend paused. "It's...fuck. You make me explain the weirdest shit. Come on."

"Weird?" I could feel Ryland's eyes on me as I reached the end of the aisle.

As I turned, I looked back, too curious to miss seeing him one last time. Ryland was watching me as his friend just stood there shaking his head. Curiosity seemed to be the only thing on his face. The guileless expression made me want to pull him into my arms and do wicked things to him.

Forcing myself to walk away and toward the other end of the store to give them some space, I heard Ryland's voice one last time. "What do you mean 'weird shit'?"

How was I supposed to stay away from perfection like that?

UNLOADING THE GROCERIES, I GLANCED OVER AT Ryland's house as I carried in another bag. Outside was quiet, but I knew that inside it had to be a flurry of last-minute preparations. Ryland's parents had been planning the trip for months and now that they were on the countdown to leave, the final plans had to be stressful.

Neither were ready to retire completely, but the vacation was their way of taking things a little bit easier and rewarding themselves for strong careers. And to a degree, I thought it was a celebration of their parenting duties ending.

Not that they'd said anything specific, but their excitement had been almost palpable.

Two more trips to my car had everything in the house, and within minutes, it was put away. Not planning any big vacation before the summer session started had seemed like a good idea when I was up to my elbows in grading and planning, but now that the quiet had descended, I was starting to rethink that decision.

There were countless projects that needed to be addressed around the house, but my mind was still back in the grocery store. There'd been a short period when I'd questioned what I'd heard, but there was no doubting what Ryland had said. The innocent excitement, the sound in his voice when he'd talked about the baby cookies, the little things his friend had said...they all added up to someone who was perfect for the lifestyle.

But it was clear he had no idea.

Walking over to the window that looked out over the back yard, I had to smile. I had a feeling his friend would be explaining some things to him very shortly, though. I found that sweet confusion enticing, but his friend clearly didn't.

How would Ryland react?

If he knew he was a bottom, then it was clear he'd had a little bit of experience, but it was also clear that his porn was fairly vanilla if he had no idea how his little comments came across. With most guys, I wouldn't have been able to understand how they were that lost by the time they'd reached college, but after meeting his parents, it was easy to see.

The Type-A planners he'd grown up with would never have let him wander off the path they had laid out for him. His time from dawn to dusk had probably been scheduled out in excruciating detail and every little thing carefully monitored. His mother might not have been planning on having children, but she wasn't the type of person who would drop the ball on an important project.

Yes...the more I thought about it, the easier it was to see why Ryland would be drawn to the carefree part of being little. I just wasn't sure if he would see it that way. It would really come down to how his friend presented it.

From the surprised look on his face, Ryland's friend knew what I'd been hinting at, but it hadn't given me enough of a clue about how he felt...or more especially how he thought the lifestyle would fit Ryland.

I'd met the young man once in the grocery store and heard him in their yard several times. There was no reason I should have been so enamored of the boy—but I'd been single too long to want to fight it. Boys who were perfect for the lifestyle didn't just show up every day, and sweet, sexy boys who made me want to pull them close were even harder to find.

As ridiculous as it would sound, I knew I wanted a chance to get to know Ryland better. But my chances of that could be rapidly dwindling, depending on how a conversation somewhere across town was going.

Unexpected
Coming June 2018

Made in the USA
Middletown, DE
05 November 2018